The Pharaoh
and the Shabti

By Michael J. Lowis

ALSO BY MICHAEL J. LOWIS

The Gospel Miracles: What Really Happened? (2014)

Euthanasia, Suicide, and Despair: Can the Bible Help? (2015)

Ageing Disgracefully, With Grace (2016)

Twenty Years in South Africa: An Immigrant's Tale (2017)

What Do We Know About God? Evidence from the Hebrew Scriptures (2017)

Reincarnation: An Historical Novel Spanning 4,000 Years (2018)

From the Pope to Pigeons; From Dreams to Heaven: Twenty Essays & Anecdotes (2018)

What's it All About, Then? Observation on Life and the Changing Times (2019)

Two Mikes and Their 39 Stories (2020) (as co-author)

Djoser and the Gods (2022)

Contents

Chapter 1

The Mission

"Hey shabti, come over here, I want to talk to you."

It was my master, Pharaoh Senusret, calling me. He is not a polite man, but my destiny is to do his bidding in perpetuity according to my appointed function. My name is not Shabti, although I am *a* shabti. He belittles me by using this term instead of my given name, which is Metjen. This means 'the leader', and my role is to lead groups of my fellows. I've been proud to do my best during my service here to justify this epithet.

"I'm coming, sir," I replied, hurrying across the square toward the palace steps where he was standing. Although I did not exist when he was ruler of Egypt in his earthly life now, in this Field of Reeds paradise created for the dead, my fellow shabtis and I have learned about him from others who knew him then.

I bowed before the Pharaoh. "How can I be of service to you, my lord?"

"We need more excitement here," he said. "In my mortal existence I was a warrior, and led expeditions northwards into the Levant and south into Nubia to suppress the uprisings against my rule. We have no enemies here, and nobody to fight. I am bored."

"Indeed sir, I've heard that you were a skilful general, and successful in your battles" I replied, trying not to sound ingratiating.

"Good, then you will know what I desire – some action!"

It was not my place to question the Pharaoh's wishes, even though my conscience told me he was wrong to want to introduce violence here where everything is provided for us. But I had to be careful what I said if I was not to be on the receiving end of his wroth. "My lord, have you forgotten what the great God Osiris and the forty-two judges said when they weighed your heart to decide if your life had been worthy? I've been told the decision to allow your soul to be rowed here across the Lake of Flowers was not unanimous."

"I am well aware of this, Metjen, and that there were conditions, but I do not need you to tell me this," Senusret replied in a no-nonsense voice.

Well, at least he has remembered my name this time. "Sir, what do you wish me to do?" I asked, hoping that he did not expect me to perform any act of aggression."

"Despite your undesirable habit of trying to lecture me, I have seen from your actions that you have leadership qualities in keeping with the meaning of your name. I therefore appoint you as my Vizier. I want you to visit the four corners of this land and seek out any behaviour that may indicate a crime or disturbance to the peace of this place. In your new senior role, nobody will question why you are carrying out this tour of inspection on my behalf."

It was an honour to be promoted to Vizier, but I knew Senusret was giving it to me as a bribe so that I'd do as he wished. "Thank you for your confidence in me, my lord," I said. "I shall go immediately and prepare to carry out your instructions. When I have something to report, I will come back and tell you."

I returned to the dwelling I shared with three other shabtis to plan my tour. Of course the Pharaoh was wrong in his desire to do battle. If Osiris and the judges find out he's not willing to live in peace with his neighbours, then he'll suffer the fate of all those found to be unworthy. He'll have his heart thrown to the floor and eaten by Ammut, the female devourer of the dead. It would be a difficult task to show him I was doing his bidding, whilst trying to ensure that nobody suffers at his hand. As it was growing dark, I decided to wait until morning before starting my journey.

Whilst resting, I went over in my mind everything I'd learned about the Pharaoh since I was created to serve him.

Senusret was the third Pharaoh of this name to hold the position of supreme leader of Egypt. When he died nearly two thousand years before what you call the Christian Era, he was mummified according to the ancient procedure. His body was then interred in the pyramid he had built for himself in the desert at Dahshur. The people believed that, when they died, their lives did not end at that moment but continued in another realm. But they needed workers to help them there and, the more important the individual, the more of them they had.

As ruler of the whole country, Senusret was entitled to have many helpers to accompany him on his journey. I was one of a host of those created to serve him. We are called shabtis. Some of us are miniature versions of our masters but I'm glad I was spared my Pharaoh's down-turned mouth, large ears and bulging eyes. We are made from wood, pottery or, as in my case, hand-carved from stone. Once the craftsmen declare they can make no further improvements to their handiwork, we are placed inside the tombs of those considered worthy. For me it was in that of the Pharaoh who was now sending me out on this mission.

But please don't think of us as mere inanimate dolls. We would be no use to anyone if that were so. Just as the deceased will rise to new life, we would also be granted the same gift and be destined to serve. However, we are not all the same. Servants had individual skills when working for their leaders when they were alive and so, in the afterlife, we shabtis are each given roles that paralleled them. They are not just random allocations, but are determined by a spell that is specified in the *Egyptian Book of the Dead*. It was a privilege for me to be considered worthy as a leader, and Sensuret has acknowledged this by the title he bestowed upon me today.

* * *

The following day, as the sun rose into the heavens, I bade farewell to my house companions and commenced my journey. Although I'd be travelling on my own, I didn't feel to be alone. Shabtis are not like Pharaohs and other important people who have the privilege of being mummified, we are just humble models. But there is camaraderie among us, and we try to help and support each other. I was sure my friends would assist me in my mission, whilst at the same time trying to ensure that the peace of this place will be preserved.

As I embarked on my tour of the Field of Reeds, its sights, sounds and smells filled me with delight and brought joy to my heart. The creator of this land certainly knew the meaning of paradise. Everyone is in the prime of their life, and people are reunited with loved ones who had passed on before. One's favourite animals are here too.

It is made up of a series of islands covered in rushes that give it its name, and each one has its own specialism. My home is on Arable Island. Whilst in many ways it's a mirror image of what the inhabitants have left behind in their mortal lives, it is an ideal place where crops always grow abundantly and trees bear succulent fruit. Everything we need for our comfort is here.

In order to ensure some level of governance, each island has a senior official appointed from among the resurrected ones and Senusret holds that position here. Rather than being dictators, their role is to guide, help and resolve any difficulties that might disturb the intended purpose of this peaceful afterlife. If anyone causes trouble to their neighbour it is the leader's job to resolve it. That is the function my master appears to be taking more earnestly than perhaps he might do.

But there are also dangers and everyone must be alert to these. At night the Field becomes the playground of the gods. The evil dead rise up and the enemies of the Supreme God Ra, creator of the world, try to defeat him so that the sun would not rise the next morning. Osiris, the God of Death and Resurrection who rules the underworld, has his home on one of the islands. My master Sensuret must have forgotten this when he asked me to seek out his foes. If Osiris discovers what the Pharaoh's intentions were, he'll quickly be taken away and re-interred in his sarcophagus, or suffer an even worse fate.

I would need to find shelter each night, both for my own protection and to reduce the chances of the purpose of my mission being discovered. But it was now morning and I had the whole day to go about my business before worrying about the dark hours. As I walked along the path that leads across the island where my Pharaoh lived, the smells of the countryside conveyed by the gentle breeze entered my nostrils, and the playful gossiping of many colourful birds entertained my ears. Blossoms decorated the fruit trees and, in the distance, I could see a wooden plough being pulled by oxen swishing their tails whilst being urged on by two worker shabtis.

A little further on I came to a small river. As I walked along its banks I saw men casting nets in the water to catch Nile perch and catfish. But these were not always servants fishing for essential foodstuffs. Some were resurrected ones who were enjoying a leisurely day in the open air with their friends. From the tone of their chatter, they appeared to be happy and contented. So far everything looked peaceful and with no hint of rebellion. It made me worried that, if this is an example of the situation throughout the land, I would have nothing to report to my warmongering master.

I continued to follow the river and, by noon, arrived at the estuary where it fed its waters into the sea. Pushing my way through the tall reeds that lined the shore, I came to a landing stage where a few small boats were tied up for citizens wishing to row across the open water to the next island. After walking for three hours I needed a rest and something to eat. There were always things to gather in this paradise and I soon harvested some nuts and fruit from nearby trees to satisfy my hunger. Sparkling water scooped from the river adequately quenched my thirst.

Whilst stretched out in the glorious sunshine for a few minutes to allow my lunch to settle, I became aware of approaching voices. If this was a party of resurrected ones and they saw me not working, I'd be in trouble. I quickly stood up, smoothed my clothing and started to make my way to one of the boats. The voices were now much closer; I turned to see who would emerge from the reeds. A group of six individuals carrying sacks appeared and walked toward the landing stage. When they saw me they cheerfully waved. I was relieved to see they were not of the privileged class but were shabti workers just like me.

Although I say 'like me', two of them were females. Yes, shabtis are not all men; women are also needed, especially by the royal princesses to attend to their cosmetic routines and care for any of their offspring who were unfortunate to die in infancy during their earthly existence. But they also become wives and companions to male shabtis, although they do not themselves bear children.

Just like I had done earlier, the group settled themselves down on the grass to rest and take refreshment. This would be a good opportunity for me to chat with others about their quality of life here. But I'd need to be careful not to reveal the true reason for my questions.

"Greetings my friends," I said, walking across to where they were sitting. "My name is

Metjen and I'm a servant of Pharaoh Senusret the third."

A distinguished-looking man with clean-shaven face and wearing a smooth skullcap rose to his feet. He came over to where I was standing. "And greetings to you, Metjen the leader. I am Bebi and I was created in the image of the chancellor who was my master. By coincidence we serve our senior official, Queen Nefret, who was the second wife of your Pharaoh's father."

"Then we are indeed kindred spirits," I replied with a smile. "Where are you heading?"

Bebi pointed to the sacks. "We've been collecting supplies of food for our community, and are taking back ears of corn, green vegetables, onions, figs and dates. When we've rested, we shall row over to our home on the next island."

"That's also where I am going," I replied.

"And may I ask what your mission is there," he asked.

"The Pharaoh has instructed me to explore regions of this land that he has not yet visited, and then report back to him" I said, hoping this did not sound too general. "I was about to row over to your island just before you arrived."

This seemed to satisfy Bebi, at least for the present. "Then we can go together, and I shall be pleased to give you a tour of our homeland once we have delivered these food items."

"Thank you, that would be most helpful, but please first complete your meal and enjoy your rest; I'm in no hurry."

A short while later I helped my new friends to load their sacks onto the boats, and we rowed across the stretch of water that separated the two islands. Two hours later, as we marched along the path toward the palace where Queen Nefret lived, Bebi said: "By the time we've delivered these items and made our way to our own home, it will be growing dark. As you know, it's important we are all indoors before the gods come down and commence their nightly arguments. You are most welcome to stay with us tonight in safety, and we can then begin our tour of the island tomorrow."

* * *

Although we shabtis are here to serve our superiors, we don't have to live like slaves but are provided with comfortable homes here in this paradise. My new companions lived together in the same big house located within the spacious grounds of the palace, so it was a good opportunity to get to know them better and gain their confidence. We'd only just completed our evening meal when the noise outside started. Thankful that the sturdy door was secured, we peeped through the small gaps between the window shutters.

The God Ra, with the sun symbol displayed proudly on the top of his hawk's head, had completed his journey across the sky where he brought light to the world. He was now locked in combat with the evil snake Apophis, God of Chaos and Darkness. If Ra didn't defeat it, the sun would not rise tomorrow. So far he'd always managed to win but the day might yet come when he fails to do so. We then caught sight of Amon, the God of Air, join in the battle. He was trying to help Ra but then the dog-like Seth, God of Violence and Storms, leapt onto Amon's back, knocked off his plumed crown and tried to bite his neck.

Soon many more deities passed by our vantage point, mostly too quickly for me to recognise. After an hour of this mayhem the noise thankfully started to recede as the warring party moved on to other parts of this land. We could only hope that, just like on all the other nights so far, Ra and his allies would be victorious and we shall have light again tomorrow.

There was now an opportunity to enjoy the company of my new friends and engage in some conversation that might help me in my mission. But it was Bebi who spoke first. "Tell me something about this Pharaoh of yours. You were created to serve him so you'll know far more about him than we do."

"Certainly," I replied, pleased that my host was keen to chat. "In his previous existence my master was not a cheerful man. His face usually displayed a sombre expression and his eyes protruded from hollow sockets. He wanted the people to see him as strict and with everything under his control, so that they would obey his wishes without question."

Bebi nodded. "Yes, we've seen images that do portray him in this way. But was he a man of peace, or of aggression?"

"Mostly aggression," I said, remembering what he'd told me when he sent me on this mission. "His great ambition was to expand his kingdom, and he did so by invading surrounding territories including Nubia and Canaan. After his victories he proclaimed that any of his descendents who failed to fight and maintain these boundaries would be disowned."

"He certainly sounds to be a man who enjoys physical combat," Bebi commented. "With such a military background, life must be very dull for him here despite all the comforts that it offers."

Was this just the opportunity I was hoping for to reveal the purpose behind my mission, I wondered? Or would it be too soon to show my hand to these people I only met earlier today?

I needed to be careful in case they were not quite as innocent as they seemed, and were obliged to report any potential acts of rebellion that would disturb the idyllic life-style here.

"You may be right, but this is a peaceful place and there are no enemies to fight, at least not unless you are one of the gods who squabble all night."

The short pause that followed before Bebi spoke again made me wonder if he was also trying to decide if he should disclose information that could land him in trouble. "Yes, this land was created to provide relief from the constant troubles and conflicts of earthly life. But my friends and I have been here longer than you have, and we have encountered some individuals who have brought their conflicts with them."

"I'm surprised to hear this," I said. "Do you think it could escalate into open warfare, or will they eventually forgive and forget and just enjoy all that has been provided for them in this place?"

"My guess is that the dissatisfaction will not go away, and that open hostility will eventually break out. Beliefs, feelings and ambitions don't die with human beings when they come to the end of their mortal lives; they remain with them when they're transported to this after-life. If someone discovers that their earthly foe is also here, there's a good chance they may seize any opportunity to complete what they regard as unfinished business."

I would soon have to decide whether to continue this verbal jousting, or reveal the exact purpose of my mission. Perhaps hold back for a while longer, just to be sure, I thought. "This doesn't seem to be the perfect paradise that I expected," I said. "Thank you for opening my eyes to the reality of the Field of Reeds. Do you perhaps have an example you can share with me of this pot that one day might boil over?"

Again Bebi hesitated. He must be starting to suspect there was a purpose behind my probing.

Eventually he answered. "Yes, I can, but such information can be dangerous in the wrong hands. If Osiris finds out that the tranquillity of the afterlife he created for us is going to be disrupted, he might bring it to an end for everybody. Is that what we want, Metjen?"

It became clear that the time had now come for me to be honest with my new friends, as they appeared to be being with me. "Of course we need to be very careful, but there's something I must tell you before we go any further. Whilst it's true my master sent me out to explore regions of this land he has not yet visited himself, he specifically requires me to seek out any signs of trouble or aggression that threatens the peace."

"I did wonder if there was more to your

travels than just sight-seeing," Bebi said. "Tell me, if your Pharaoh does find what he is seeking, what does he intend to do about it?"

"He didn't spell it out in detail," I replied, "But Senusret said he was bored and desired some action. He was a general in his earthly life and it seems he wishes to be one here in paradise."

By the look on Bebi's face I could see he was worried. "If he just wants to gallop off with his private army and start killing people, it would be a risk to all of us. Certainly Osiris would not just stand aside and let this happen. We must prevent upsetting our Creator God or we shall all suffer the consequences. What do you propose to do, Metjen, if you do discover some of your Pharaoh's enemies?"

I knew that, if I indicated I'd simply report this to Senusret and then let him go off to fight, Bebi and his friends would make sure I would never leave this house again. Fortunately, I was as unhappy with what my master commanded me to do as were my hosts, so I could speak frankly. "When I was informed of my mission, I knew he was wrong and did try to point out Osiris might take revenge on him for trying to upset the peace of this afterlife."

"And what did he say to that?"

"He told me not to lecture him, but to just go

and carry out his orders. He tried to pacify me by promoting me to Vizier."

"So what will you tell him if you do find some of his old adversaries?"

"I certainly don't want to report back anything that will give him the excuse to go off and fight, and yet I can't just tell lies. For all I know he might have appointed spies to check on me, or even others to also do what I am doing. I haven't yet worked out what I could do that would avoid trouble in either one direction or another."

Bebi remained quiet for a few moments. "There may be a way," he eventually announced.

"And what is that?"

"If someone takes up arms to fight those who are trying to disrupt or destroy what Osiris has created, then surely the God would look on him with favour."

"This is indeed something we could consider," I conceded. "You said earlier you'd come across people who had brought their grievances with them, and would not hesitate to use aggression to try and resolve them here. But you hesitated in giving me an example."

"Now that you've disclosed the true purpose behind your expedition, I feel assured you are not a spy sent to cause trouble for us," Bebi said, now looking more relaxed. "We did recently encounter a group of people who were constantly complaining about how they had been treated during their earthly existence, and who might want to take revenge here. You may be interested to know that this involves your Pharaoh's family."

I was shocked to hear this. Whilst my master had the reputation of being a warrior king my understanding was that, for almost one hundred years, the monarchs who preceded him were lovers of peace. "Thank you for your confidence in me, Bebi, but please tell me what you know about this."

"All right, here it is. We've learned that, during the first year of the reign of your Pharaoh's father, Senusret the Second, a man called Joseph from Canaan was sold by into slavery in Egypt by his brothers. He was the favourite of his father Jacob, who gave him a coat of many colours, but his brothers were jealous of his ability to analyse dreams."

"Yes, I have heard of this man," I commented. "But I always thought he was a well-respected person and not one to incite a rebellion."

Bebi continued. "Just keep in mind the word I used: 'jealousy' and I'll come back to it shortly. Joseph soon found favour but, through no fault of his own, was soon in trouble again. But whilst languishing in prison in Egypt, his reputation as an interpreter of dreams reached Pharaoh Senusret the Second. He was released after correctly predicting that a famine would follow seven years of good harvest. This enabled the Pharaoh to store enough grain to see the nation through the lean years."

"So far nothing you've told me suggests that this Joseph was anything other than a righteous individual. I still don't understand what this has to do with our current issue."

"I'm just coming to that," Bebi said. "You must be patient, Metjen, if you want to truly understand. Senusret was so pleased with Joseph that he appointed him as his Viceroy, and he became a powerful figure second only to the Pharaoh himself. And this is where I come back to the word 'jealousy'."

"Ah, do mean there were those who were jealous of Joseph's elevated position?"

"Exactly that. There were many senior officials who had aspired to that important role at court, and the fact that it was given to a foreigner was bitterly resented. The Pharaoh was content to leave most of the decisions to Joseph whilst he enjoyed a life of peace with his family. Those who felt they'd been passed over were not able to take their revenge on him during his earthly life because he was well protected. However, during our travels we've heard there are several of them in this land who wish to do so now."

This was very useful information, and I spent a few moments considering it before speaking.

"It appears from what you say that Joseph was successful in being admitted to this paradise, as were some of the officials who resented him. Do you know which part of this land they inhabit?"

"To answer your first question, yes, Joseph is here as are some of the Pharaoh's staff members who had been mummified and entombed. Their hearts had been weighed by Osiris, and they were judged worthy to be admitted. But many of the officials failed the test. They were therefore left to the mercy of the God Ammut and now cease to exist. With regard to your second question. No, we don't know where these people are at this time."

"The Field of Reeds has many islands, and it could take months or even years to explore them all," I said. "If I'm unable to report back to my Pharaoh for such a long time, he might think I have deserted him and then lead a hunting party to find me. I shall just have to set off early tomorrow morning and quickly travel as far and wide as I can."

Bebi's face displayed a broad smile. "You are starting to panic, my friend. Calm down a bit.

We might be able to help you. I did say earlier that we would be pleased to show you our own island, and perhaps we might be able to do more than this."

I now felt embarrassed that I'd reacted so quickly without first discussing the situation a bit more. "Sorry Bebi," I said. "You are being so helpful and I am reacting without thinking. What do you have in mind?"

"It's now late, and we all need to rest," he replied. "You are our guest, so let's sleep safely in this house tonight. We can discuss our plans in the morning – assuming of course that Ra wins his battle again and climbs back into the heavens to give us light."

Chapter 2

The Journey Begins

The next morning, with the sun shining brightly where it belonged, my hosts insisted on avoiding any further discussions until we had completed our first meal of the day. We then sat outside and enjoyed a gentle, cooling breeze on our faces, bringing with it fragrant scents from the gardens that surrounded Queen Nefret's palace. I tried to be patient, but the urge to discover what my hosts were planning for me eventually triumphed. "Bebi, you and your friends have been most kind in extending your hospitality to me. Last night you hinted you might be able to help me further in my mission, and I'm very keen to hear what you have in mind."

"Of course, Metjen, I didn't mean to keep you waiting but I first had to check with others on a few details. The Queen whom we serve allows us to follow our own activities provided we keep the palace larder stocked with food. What we delivered yesterday will be sufficient for two weeks. This means that at least some of us will have the opportunity to go away for this length of time."

I had a suspicion of what was to come, but just smiled and nodded rather than interrupt.

Bebi continued. "My proposal is that three of us stay here to make sure any requests from the palace can be honoured, and the other three accompany you on a tour of as much of this land as is possible in the time available to us. We are more familiar with some parts of it than you are, but there's still much we have not yet explored. In addition to helping you, we shall be educating ourselves."

"I'm delighted you are prepared to do this," I replied, trying not to overdue my excitement. "This will help me to achieve much more than what I could do on my own. But are you sure you are willing to do this for someone you only met for the first time yesterday?"

"We've agreed you are trustworthy, and it's important for all of us that you succeed in your mission," Bebi said. "Yes, we are willing. But I must warn you that if you have not found what you are seeking by the time we have to return, you will either have to continue on your own, or come back with us knowing you have failed."

"I do understand, and will remain forever grateful to you and your friends. What I shall do if I can't report something useful to my Pharaoh will have to wait until our tour is over."

"Right, just wait until we've packed some food for today. Each day we shall need to gather what we need as well as find shelter at night from the warring gods."

A short while later we set off, and Bebi introduced me to the other two members of our little band of explorers. Intef was modelled after the court official he was created to serve. His tall stature and muscular physique indicated he would be a useful man to have with you when danger threatened. Completing our quartet was Khumit, a female modelled in the likeness of a beautiful princess whose earthly life was prematurely ended by illness. With her long black hair and finely chiselled features, she now served the island's senior official, Queen Nefret.

Whilst all of the islands in this paradise were beautiful, I was discovering just how different they were. The one where I lived had abundant food crops, and this is why my new friends visited it to collect supplies for the palace. Flowers were common to all, but we were now walking through fields of blossoms of every shape and colour, their fragrances enveloping us as if we had been bathed in the most expensive perfume. The noise of thousands of bees entertained our ears whilst they gorged themselves on the copious supplies of sweet nectar. It's not surprising it was given the name Flower Island.

Bebi and Intef were leading the way, with Khumit and me following. "With all those bees, there must be much honey available here," I said to my lady companion.

"Indeed there is," she confirmed. "We need to come to your island for the crops that grow, but we can collect as much honey as we need right here. In fact we shall do so when it comes time to eat, to put on the bread we have brought with us."

"I shall look forward to that; it's making me hungry just thinking about it," I said.

Khumit's laugh at my comment was like the tinkling of bells, as she bent down to collect a small posy of blooms and pushed them into her headband. We continued to chat as we walked along, and I had almost forgotten that this was not a pleasure trip but a serious mission that had to achieve its purpose. I called out to my host and guide. "Bebi, this is a beautiful place but we have not yet seen anybody to talk with."

"You are again being impatient, my friend," he replied. "This is not a highly populated island, and we know most of the inhabitants here. In any event I doubt they'll have anything useful to tell us. We'll reach the sea by mid day and can then rest and refresh ourselves. Just enjoy the beauty of this place whilst you have the chance. This afternoon we'll cross over to the next island. We've seldom visited it before, but we'll try to meet some of the people there and question them".

Of course Bebi was correct in urging patience, but we only had two weeks for this expedition and it was important for me to make some progress quickly if I'm not to tell Senusret I've failed. Just as predicted, we reached the sea as the sun was at its zenith. Whilst Intef went off to collect some honey, Khumit unpacked the bread and fruit we had brought with us. We were soon enjoying our meal and resting our legs as we sat on the grassy bank near the shore.

In common with my own island, small boats were tied up by a jetty. The creator of this place certainly provided for all the needs of its inhabitants. My day-dreaming was disturbed by Bebi's voice: "If we wish to explore the next island and then find somewhere to shelter for the night, we should be moving on without delay."

We climbed into one of the boats and set off. By mid afternoon we made landfall and started to walk inland. This island was different again from the two I'd already experienced as it had the greatest variety of animals. In the first few minutes alone we saw gazelles, baboons, monkeys and jackals. But not all the creatures here were friendly. Away in the distance we even spied a lion stalking through the trees. Cows and goats were grazing contentedly in fields that had been fenced off, and we could also see a large pond populated with ducks and geese constantly bobbing their heads beneath the surface looking for food. It was aptly named Animal Island.

After two hours of brisk walking without seeing anyone, we reached the middle of the island and came to a farmhouse with several outbuildings. "Bebi," I said. "Shall we go up to the house and talk with the people there? We might learn something that'll help us in our quest."

As we were making our way along the drive the door opened and two shabtis wearing farming smocks came out to meet us, followed by a large brown dog. "Greetings," Bebi said. "We do not mean to intrude, but we are from Flower Island on a mission of exploration."

The camaraderie between shabtis was again evident by the response. "Welcome my friends, I am Shakir. This is my wife Bennu and our dog Tut. Can we be of service to you?"

"That is most kind of you," Bebi replied, introducing each of us. "We've not been here before, and you are the first locals we have met. We were just hoping you might be able to tell us a little about the people who live on your island."

"Certainly; we shall be glad to," Shakir said warmly. "We were just having a short break before it's time to milk our cows again. Please come inside and join us for some beer whilst we talk."

We were pleased to accept their invitation, and went into their house. Whilst not being luxurious, the furnishings were comfortable and adequate to fulfil all the needs of those who lived there. Once we had settle down with a beaker of the local brew, our host asked, "What is it you would like to know from us?"

Again we needed to be cautious, just like it was before admitting to my new friends the true purpose of my mission. There was always the possibility that someone might want to make sure we failed in our quest, or even that we disappeared completely. But Bebi knew how tread carefully. "We're keen to learn more about those who passed the test set by Osiris and the judges after they reached the end of their earthly lives, and were then admitted to this Field of Reeds."

Shakir stroked his short beard. He didn't answer directly, but responded with a question of his own. "As you know, there are more shabtis here than those who were reincarnated. Who is it that you were created to serve in the afterlife?"

I considered it prudent to answer first, as I did not want my friends to be comprised trying to explain my presence. "My master is Pharaoh Senusret the third, and I am from the island where the arable crops grow."

"Ah, so you are not from the Flower Island like your companions," Shakir responded, patting his dog. "Did you decide to take this pleasure trip to visit old friends?"

Our host was certainly being cautious, and I wondered if he'd previously found himself in trouble by saying too much. But it was still too soon to be completely open about the true reason for our presence. "Oh no," I said with a laugh. "We only met each other for the first time yesterday. Senusret was keen to learn more about this paradise but, rather than embark on a journey of exploration himself, he asked me to do so and then report back to him."

"We've heard a little about the reputation of your master," Shakir commented. "He doesn't exactly come across as a man of peace. But what of you, Bebi, Intef and Khumit – were you charged with the same mission?"

I was about to answer, but Bebi intervened. "Again no," he said. "As Metjen mentioned we only met yesterday but, when he told us about his assignment, we decided to join him. There is much we ourselves do not know about this land."

Shakir was proving to be someone you could not satisfy with just simple responses, and I was starting to worry that we might be being too trusting too quickly. Although we shabtis always tried to help each other, there was always the possibility that some had been recruited as spies to ensure there was no unexpected rebellion. "Were you granted leave from your duties to join Metjen in what could become a long trip?" he said, addressing Bebi.

"We can only be away a short time from Queen Nefret, whom we serve. After we had filled the palace larder with the food we'd gathered on Metjen's island, we have two weeks before it will need replenishing. Our Queen does not trouble us so long as she and her court do not go hungry."

"I see," Shakir said. "But when we met outside the farm house a short while ago, you wanted to know something about the people here rather than the geography. Is this what Senusret specifically asked you to do, Metjen?"

This was becoming tricky, I thought. Was it too early to tell this shrewd shabti the truth? There seemed to be no alternative if we wanted his help. "You said earlier that Senusret doesn't have the reputation as being a man of peace. This is accurate. Rather than just enjoying being in this paradise that provides for his every need, he's looking for any act of rebellion he can do battle against. The aggressive part of his personality remained with him through death, mummification, and reincarnation."

"Thank you for being open about why you are here," Shakir said. "I did think there might be more to your mission than just tourist sight seeing. But I can understand your initial reticence to reveal all because this could become dangerous information if it reached the wrong ears."

Once again Bebi stepped in before I could speak. "There's something my companions and I have heard that can narrow down our search. You might know the story of Joseph, who had been abandoned by his family and was put in an Egyptian prison. He was released by the Pharaoh of that time because of his remarkable ability to interpret dreams, and eventually promoted to the leading position in court."

Shakir nodded. "Please continue."

"Well, that Pharaoh was the father of the one Metjen now serves. Many of his senior officials were very resentful to have been passed over, especially in favour of a foreigner. They could not take their revenge because Joseph was protected by the Pharaoh. However, we believe that some of them are here in this Field of Reeds and are prepared to complete what they could not do in their earthly life."

"Now that I have the full story, I think we might be able to help you," Shakir said. "We hear many things when travellers come to the farm to obtain our produce. But Metjen, if your master does receive the information he is seeking, what action will he then take?"

"It'll certainly be physical action in view of his urge to do battle," I replied. "I was bold enough to mention that Osiris might not take kindly to him disrupting this idyllic place, but he made it clear he did not relish my advice. But Bebi has suggested there might be a way to avoid this."

"Please share this with us, Bebi," Shakir asked.

"If Osiris sees any action Senusret may take as being one that prevents a more serious threat to himself and this afterlife he has created, then he is more likely to reward the Pharaoh than to punish him."

"Yes, an excellent idea," Shakir commented as everyone nodded their agreement. "I'm not sure how you'll be able to achieve this, but it can be a plan that guides you."

"Bennu, Shakir's wife had said very little up to this moment but now interrupted: "You've all been talking so much that the time for the evening milking of our herd of cows is already overdue. We can continue with this once our work is done."

"We shall be glad to help you with this," said Bebi. "You have been so kind in extending the hand of friendship to us, that it's the least we can do."

I had had no prior experience in performing this task, so my contribution was more of a hindrance than a help. By the time the job was done and the cows had been fed, it was starting to grow dark.

"Thank you all for your assistance," Shakir said once we were seated back in the farmhouse. "But we now have another problem. It would be dangerous for you continued your journey outside now, because Ra is coming to the end of his daily path across the sky. Soon the gods will be fighting again. We never know where this will be but, if it is close to us, you could be unwilling participants in the conflict – to your cost."

"You've been very helpful to us already," Bebi replied. "We would not wish to burden you with our presence any longer; I'm sure we shall survive and maybe the battle will be far away tonight."

Shakir shook his head. "No, I will not hear of you leaving now, and there's still more we need to discuss that may help you in your mission. Our house is small but the barns are large. After we have shared some refreshment you will be most welcome to take shelter in one of the outbuildings we keep for storing cattle food."

I consulted with Intef and Khumit, but it didn't take long to agree we should accept the offer of Shakir and his wife. There might well be nights to come when we would have nowhere to hide, so to be safely behind doors this time would mean one less thing to worry about. "Thank you very much," I answered on behalf of our party. If you're sure this will be no trouble to you, we would be delighted to accept your kind invitation."

"Good, that is settled then," Shakir said. "Let us now just relax and enjoy some food, and then I can tell you something that may help you.

* * *

Shakir and Bennu were generous hosts. Not only did they serve produce from their own farm, but also bread, vegetables and fruit imported from the other islands. Several goblets of the beer they had brewed themselves completed a very satisfying meal.

Once the feasting was over and the oil lamps had been lit, I said to our hosts: "That was most enjoyable and much better than we would have been able to prepare for ourselves had we been outside. Thank you both. Now Shakir, you said earlier you had information that might help us in our mission. Would you like to share this with us now?"

"Yes, I shall not keep you waiting any longer. Two weeks ago three noblemen knocked at our door and said they were seeking information. They were not shabtis like us, but had lived an earthly life and been resurrected. Because they were men of authority, we respectfully invited them inside our house to hear what they had to say. When we saw you and your party this morning, at first we thought you had the same quest, and in some ways you have."

"Please tell us what they wanted," I asked.

Bebi gave a laugh. "You'll have to forgive my friend Metjen, for he is an impatient fellow."

"I do understand," Shakir said. "If I were in his position I'd be the same. The men said they were seeking the whereabouts of a man called Joseph, who was also a resurrected one. He was the very same Joseph you spoke about earlier today."

I was shocked to her this. Surely Senusret would not have sent out someone else to carry out the same mission as I had been given. Before I had chance to say something, Bebi said, "This is quite a coincidence. Before we met Metjen we heard that some people were intent on seeking revenge against Joseph for depriving them of the chance to be promoted to senior positions in court."

"Well it seems we now know who it is who is trying to locate this man," said Shakir. "They even told me their names: Hepzefa, Neferu and Simontu."

"Were you able to give them any information?" I asked.

"No. We don't know where this Joseph lives, but we do know that these three officials come from the next island in this group, the one with all the lakes teaming with fish. When we told them we had no knowledge of Joseph's whereabouts, they left but not before sternly instructing us to report to them any information we might come across in the future."

"And that is where the trouble might start, so this is very useful to know." I said. "Thank you for sharing this with us."

"It's now getting late, and I think you should take one of these lamps and settle down in the barn before we hear anything from the warring gods," Shakir suggested. "We can give you some blankets to help you to be comfortable, but do be sure to bolt the door securely to prevent any intrusion during the night."

We made our way to the barn. It was quiet outside so we hoped this indicated the gods would be conducting their squabbles elsewhere in the Field of Reeds tonight. After we'd each found a spot in the hay where we could spread our blankets, Bebi and I checked that the door had been securely bolted. "Shall we keep the lamp burning? I asked my friend.

"Perhaps it would be a good idea to do so," he suggested, wrapping his blanket around himself. "This is not a familiar building to us and we may need to get up during the night to check that all is well." I could only agree with him, and settled down to rest, now realising just how tired I was.

I don't know for how long I was asleep, but was suddenly awakened by a loud rattling noise.

It was coming from high up in the barn. The lamp was weakly flickering, trying to survive on the last few drops of the oil; without it there would be complete darkness unless we unbarred the door and admitted some of the pale moonlight. Bebi was also starting to emerge from his slumbers, and I whispered to him. "What's all that noise coming from above? It sounds like somebody, or something is trying to force its way in here."

Now fully awake, he listened for a few moments before replying. "Yes, it does sound as if we may have an unwelcome intruder. But, from the commotion on the other side of the door, it appears that Ra is again fighting for his survival, and it's happening just outside this barn."

"I agree, but we can't risk opening the door to check. And the lamp is nearly empty; we shall soon have nothing to see by. Perhaps we should quickly have a look around the barn to try and discover the cause of the rattling."

As the other two members of our party started to awaken we walked to the back of the building, stumbling over items we couldn't see in the fading light. There, propped up in the corner, was a ladder that led up to a small loft near the roof. "Let me climb up and investigate," I said. "It sounds as if the noise could be coming from up there."

"All right, but be careful because it might be dangerous, whatever it is," Bebi replied, as we were joined by Intef and Khumit, curious to know what was going on. As I reached the platform in the dim light, I could just make out a hinged flap in the roof above it. It was secured with a bolt, but something was banging on the outside.

I shouted down to those below. "There looks to be an access to this loft through the roof, and it sounds as if somebody wants to open it."

"It might be a person stranded up there who's trying to escape from the fighting," Bebi called back. "Perhaps we should take the chance and open the hatch to let them in."

"But it could also be someone who is a danger to us," I said. "What should I do – ignore what might be a cry for help, or risk exposing our party to danger?"

"The lamp is just about to go out and you will not be able to find your way down the ladder in the dark. Do what you have to do quickly and come straight down."

In anticipation there might be someone out there who needed assistance, I decided to risk unlocking the hatch but to then quickly retreat. In what was now almost pitch darkness, we all looked up and saw the flap start to open.

Silhouetted against a background of stars we could just make out a shadowy figure climb onto the loft. The hatch closed. We heard the bolt being slid back, but could see nothing. Whomever, or whatever it was then started to make its way down the ladder. Khumit came to my side, trembling. "We are all going to die," she whispered. There was nothing I could say in comfort, but I put my arm around her and held her close. Footsteps made their way toward us.

Chapter 3

Godly Encounters

"Thank you for letting me in," said a voice mixed with squeaks that did not sound quite human. "I shall now provide you with some light to see by." A warm glow gradually illuminated the scene, and soon we could see it came from a golden orb on top of a figure with the head of a hawk. We gasped in amazement: the God Ra was standing in front of us. Immediately we all went down on one knee in the presence of this awesome being.

"Please stand up, good people," Ra requested. "I sometimes tire of these nightly battles and seek sanctuary so my adversaries cannot find me. All I ask is that I stay here for a while until Ammut, Seth, Apopis and the others who delight in trying to defeat me have moved on to other parts of the Field."

"It would indeed be an honour to shelter you for as long as you wish, my lord," said Bebi, answering on behalf of us all. "We are also grateful you are able to share a little of your light with us in here now that our lamp has run dry."

We made ourselves comfortable on the hay, greatly relieved that we were in no immediate danger. "I am surprised to find you spending the night in this barn instead of the house," Ra said.

"We are not residents of Animal Island but are visitors on a mission of exploration," I answered. "The farmer kindly offered us this accommodation for the night so we would not be outside when your antagonists began their attack on you. Tomorrow we shall continue on our journey."

"It is fortunate for me that you were here and opened the hatch, otherwise I would have had to continue fighting or find somewhere else to shelter" Ra said. "Although we are powerful, we do not break down doors for our own benefit. But I would like to hear more about the purpose of your exploration; perhaps I might be able to repay you with some help."

"My lord" I began, wondering how open I should be. "I started this trip on Arable Island at the request of my master, Senusret the Third. He asked me to visit other islands and then report back to him on what I had seen. When I reached the shore I met Bebi and his party, and he took me to his home on Flower Island. The next day he, Intef and Khumit decided to accompany me as I continued my journey, but only for two weeks."

"And then you came across the water to Animal Island?" Ra asked.

"Yes. The first people we met were Farmer Shakir and his wife Bennu. They kindly let us spend the night in their barn so we would be safe. We were awakened by your banging on the trap door in the roof."

"I am sorry I awakened you, but also pleased we have this chance to meet you all. But you have not been very specific about your assignment from the Pharaoh. There must have been some particular information he was seeking. If I am to try and help you, I would need to know what it was."

Oh dear, I thought. Here we go again. No matter how hard I attempt to hide what Senusret really wanted, I find myself having to disclose it sooner than I had intended. But perhaps I could try and phrase my answer in a more positive light. "Sir, you are correct; there was something he especially wanted me to explore. He had heard rumours there may be some residents who wish to disrupt the tranquillity of this paradise by seeking out someone they regard as their enemy, and taking revenge on him. If my master knew who these people were, he would chase after them and prevent this happening."

"I see," Ra chirped through his beak. "But it

does sound as if he wishes to use aggression to curb aggression. That would surely do little to maintain peace in this Field of Reeds."

Bebi could see I was at risk of being forced into a corner from which it would difficult to escape. "Metjen discussed this with me in detail when we first met," he said. "I had some information that was helpful to him."

"Can you tell me what that was?"

"It concerned a man called Joseph who was promoted to the royal court over the heads of others who thought they were more worthy than him. We have heard they could not take their revenge on him in their earthly life, but are intent on doing so now they are all here in paradise."

I took up the discussion again, relieved that the truth was being told. But I was also becoming concerned that the purpose of our mission was being shared with more people than it should be. If this reached the ears of those we were seeking they would no doubt make sure that they would never be found. "When we met the farmer yesterday, he had some information that was very useful. He said he had recently been visited by three men who were seeking this man Joseph, and he suspected they were the resurrected court officials who were seeking revenge."

"Thank you for being open about your mission," Ra said. "You can be confident that I shall not repeat this to anyone. During my journeys I shall keep watch for anything that might help, and then seek you out to tell you. But it is now quiet outside as my opponents have moved elsewhere trying to find me. It is time for me to leave and take up my position in the heavens so I can provide light for the world tomorrow."

We opened the barn door and let our guest depart. There was still time to resume our rest before we had to be on our way next morning, but the sleep for which our bodies craved had to compete with the excitement that lingered in our minds from the experiences of the last hour.

When the first sunbeams entering through the gaps around the door indicated that Ra had begun his day's journey across the heavens we arose, packed our belongings and went to see if the farmer and his companion were awake. We were foolish to think it might be too early, as Shakir and Bennu had already started the morning milking of their cows. Once again we did our best to help them – it was the least we could do to try and repay their hospitality.

When the churns were full and the cattle back grazing in the fields, our farming friends insisted we join them for some refreshment before we left. It was an opportunity to tell them about the events of the previous night. They were used to the noise of the fighting gods that sometimes passed by their house, but were amazed that we had actually had an encounter with Ra. "It's good that the Sun God has offered to help you, if he can," Shakir said. "If you're going to succeed in your quest you'll need all the assistance you can get."

We departed as soon as we had finished eating, warmly thanking these two hard-working farmers for their hospitality that included some extra provisions pressed upon us for our onward journey.

When I left my home on Arable Island two days ago, I had strong doubts I'd be able to return to Pharaoh Senusret with any information that would please him. Now I had already learned of a threat to Joseph and had the names of those who wished to wreak vengeance on him. If my master succeeded in preventing the murder of an innocent man, Osiris would surely be pleased rather than angry. Would I make any more progress in my mission today, I wondered?

* * *

Whilst Bebi again led the way with Intef by his side, Khumit walked along with me behind them. With her attractive face and flowing black hair with the gold band, it was easy to see she had been modelled in the image of the princess she served. "I'm so glad you were there with me last night, Metjen, as it was very frightening until Ra revealed himself," she said quietly so the others could not hear.

"But Intef is strong and powerful; he would have defended you better than I could have done should it have been necessary," I replied, feeling a little embarrassed at this unexpected compliment.

"Oh, he might be tough, which is probably why Bebi included him in our party, but he lacks judgement and compassion. He's not someone I can admire or feel is a close friend."

I decided to change the subject rather than continue with these personal revelations. "We've a mission to perform, but only a limited time in which to do it. Animal Island seems to be only sparsely populated with people because much of the land has been made available for the cows, sheep and other livestock. If we're to obtain information about Joseph and those who whish to take their revenge on him, there needs to be folk we can talk with."

"Yes, I agree," Khumit replied, smiling wistfully. "What a pity this is not just a holiday trip for both of us to enjoy without having to concern ourselves with this task."

"Bebi," I called out to our friends who by

now were several yards ahead of us. "Can you see any of the local people we can talk with?"

"There are several workers further along the road and they're coming toward us," he shouted back.

They stopped when they reached our party, and I could see they were fellow shabtis and not resurrected nobles. "Greetings, my friends," the first one said. "I am Neferti, servant of my master the priest. We don't see many strangers on this island. What brings you here?"

As with our previous encounters, we again needed to be careful but I considered it was my responsibility to answer first. "My name is Metjen from Arable Island, and my companions are from Flower Island. I serve Pharaoh Senusret, and he has sent me on a mission to explore some of the other islands in the Field of Reeds. We landed here yesterday."

"You are welcome to our place in paradise," Neferti said. "We're on our way to move a herd of cattle to fresh pasture. I hope you will be able to report favourably on our island. If you are looking for something in particular, perhaps we could help you find it."

It became clear to me that everyone we were going to speak with would want to know more about the purpose of our mission before offering information in return. This was understandable, but it was a risk we would have to take even though we needed to be careful. If the word got back to those who were seeking revenge that we were trying to stop them, then we could be the ones to receive the first blow. "Last night farmer Shakir allowed us to sleep in his barn, so that we'd be indoors when the gods commenced their fighting," I began.

"Ah yes, we know that couple well. In fact we know everyone who lives on this island," Neferti replied. "It was good that you were not outside during the night because the battle raged very close by."

"Indeed, we also heard it. But the farmer told us that three men had recently called on them to ask if they knew the whereabouts of a man called Joseph. He was unable to help them, but the visitors said he must be sure to let them know if any information came his way."

Neferti gave a knowing nod. "We were also visited by these people. In fact everyone we have met since was also asked the same question, but nobody could help them. Are you perhaps also interested in the whereabouts of this man Joseph?"

There was no alternative now; I had to trust these folk we had only just met. "Yes, it so happens we are. We believe these three travellers are intent on taking their revenge on Joseph for depriving them of the chance of promotion at the royal court."

"And are you seeking to prevent such an act of aggression?"

"In his earthly life my master Pharaoh Senusret often led his troops to suppress rebellion. Now, in his reincarnation, he would consider it his duty to do the same in this paradise."

"Did he know about Joseph and the danger he is in?" Neferti asked?

"No, he didn't mention this when he sent me out, but to just make a tour of the islands and report back to him any signs of potential trouble. It was only when I was told by Bebi, and then the farmer, that I heard about the Joseph issue for the first time. Before I say anything about this to the Pharaoh, it would be very useful to have more details."

"Sorry my friend, there is little more that I know that can help you. As I mentioned, we know everyone on Animal Island, and neither Joseph nor the three men live here. This might save you wasting your time exploring, but I'm unable to suggest where you should go next."

Bebi had kept silent up to this point, but he now responded on behalf of our group. "Thank you for this, Neferti, we shall proceed to the coast without delay and take the boat to the next island."

"It's always a pleasure to meet fellow workers from other parts of this land, and I wish you success in your mission," Neferti replied. "But there's something else I can tell you. We have observed that the lions are heading this way, and we're going to keep vigil on our animals throughout the night so we can repel any attempts to attack them. You might want to make sure you are in a safe place if you cannot leave here before morning."

We bid them farewell and continued along the road. "Do you know how far it is to the sea?" I asked Bebi.

"No, I'm not familiar with this island but it appears to be larger than those we have visited before. Let's hope we reach it before it is dark, or maybe find shelter if we do not."

We walked on trying to maintain a brisk pace, but it only made us need to stop and rest more often. Once again Khumit came close to me as we walked. "I didn't think we would have to face wild animals," she said. "It's a frightening prospect and I'm worried we might not reach the coast in time."

I put my hand on her arm, trying to reassure her. "The sun is still high, and it's too soon to start worrying. We must just keep going and hope that we shall remain safe."

After another two hours of walking without seeing any other person we stopped to eat the last of the provisions we had brought with us. Bebi clambered up onto a small mound so he could look further into the distance. "I still can't see the coastline, so it's unlikely we shall reach it before night time. Let's keep going until Ra's journey is nearly done, and then make camp with whatever we can find." There was no alternative but to agree with him, so we wearily raised ourselves up and continued along the road.

At last we came across some more local inhabitants. Two workers were repairing a fence that had been knocked over by something or someone, allowing their livestock to stray from their field. They had a small ox cart with them containing new posts, rope and other equipment they might need for their task. "Greetings," Bebi said. "We are hoping to reach the coast before nightfall. Can you tell us how far away it is?"

"It's four hours journey from here," one of them replied. "In another two hours the sun will have disappeared and you will not want to be walking in the dark, especially when the lions might be prowling."

This was not good news, but we bade them farewell and continued on as fast as our tired legs would carry us. By late afternoon the light was fading. We had not encountered any other people nor had we seen any building that might provide us with the protection we would need until morning. It was time we stopped walking and discussed our situation. "What are we to do?" Khumit asked, making an effort to keep her voice steady.

"We've no alternative but to sleep outside tonight," Bebi replied. "Let's look around to see if we can find anything that might protect us."

"There are no animals in the field on our left, so we could at least go behind the fence," I said.

"It looks like the workers we saw earlier had also been carrying out some maintenance here. Perhaps there might be some of the old wooden posts lying around that they've now replaced with new ones." We spread out and searched in the long grass.

"I've found something," Intef shouted out. "Just as you said, there is a pile of old timber along with short lengths of rope. It looks like they have been stacked up ready to be collected when the cart comes this way again."

We carried the pieces of wood to a corner of the field and used a big stone to hammer as many of them as we could into the ground near a corner where the two fences met, to form a triangle. Although this little enclosure would not protect us from the warring gods if they came our way, it might help to hold back any wild animals that creep up on us. We went inside, taking some bits of wood that we had sharpened to a point with the knife Intef had thoughtfully brought with him.

Once it was completely dark, we agreed on a rota to keep watch whilst the rest of our group lay down in the long grass to try and get some sleep. I was the first on duty, and sat down with one of the sharpened sticks next to me. It all seemed quiet and peaceful. Looking upwards the stars appeared to be shining with extra brightness, or was it just that I'd rarely just sat and gazed at them like I was now doing? There was no sign or sight of the nightly battles, so I hoped the gods had chosen some other part of this land to fight tonight.

It was an effort to stay awake, but I was suddenly alerted by a rustling sound in the grass just outside our makeshift fence.

Was this a dangerous animal trying to quietly creep up on us? My heart was beating faster as I grabbed the stick and stood up to investigate. Should I awaken the others? Their exhaustion was allowing them to enjoy some much needed sleep. No, not yet, I decided. The moon had now risen to provide a little light for me to look into the field. Peering into the distance I saw something moving.

It was too small to be a lion, but perhaps it could still be dangerous. Only when it came closer could I see it was a mongoose. This sacred creature with brindled, cat-like body and thick tail was clearly looking for prey. I knew that their menu included snakes, so it was doing us a service by checking our campsite to grab any of these slithery creatures that might be contemplating taking a bite out of us.

Leaving our friendly mongoose to enjoy its hunting, I returned to my position on the grass, glad that I had not panicked and disturbed the slumbers of my colleagues. It would soon be my turn to join them and let Intef take over the next watch.

Sleep came surprisingly quickly after I had laid down, but it didn't seem a moment before I was awakened by Intef shaking my shoulder. "There's something moving in the grass nearby," he whispered so as not to disturb the others. "I might need some help if it attacks."

I quietly roused myself and joined him at our ramshackle fence. "I saw a mongoose when I was keeping watch. Are sure it is not the same creature going about its hunting?"

Intef shook his head. "It's something bigger than that, and it also has a smell. Just sniff the air over here." I did as he suggested and yes, there was a pungent odour I could not recognise, and it was coming from something nearby.

"We better wake up the others," I suggested.

"If there is danger out there we all need to be ready to move out of the way quickly." Intef agreed, and soon the rest of our band were rubbing their eyes and wondering why they had been disturbed. The yellow moon had now started to make its way across the heavens. Although we had some light to help us, we still couldn't see what was lurking just a short distance from our enclosure.

Suddenly a creature leapt with a roar toward our fence. Just as we had been warned, it was a lion. Instinctively we shrank back a yard. It pushed its body against our fence, clearly angry that this flimsy barrier was preventing it from enjoying a meal of human flesh. Intef moved forward with the pointed stick and thrust it at the animal's head, causing it to take a step back. But it then lurched forward with even more force. The old wooden posts making up our barrier started to bend.

We all shouted and struck out with all that we had. Again the lion retreated a little. Intef pulled out his knife. It would have been suicide to try and stab such a large beast with this small weapon, but he was brave enough to try it if necessary in order to save the rest of us. One more thrust at the fence by the animal and we knew it would succeed in breaking through. I doubted that any of us would still be alive a few minutes from now. We could see that it was readying itself to pounce.

The creature surged forward; this was it. But just at that moment we were blinded by a flash of light. When we were able to see again, we were amazed to make out none other than the God Ra standing there between the lion and ourselves. He pointed a finger toward the animal and a burst of energy streamed out, hitting it in the face. It gave a loud yelp and raced away until it was out of sight.

"We're surprised to see you here, but are so grateful you have saved us from that hungry beast," Bebi said, echoing the relief we all felt. "How did you know we needed help?"

"Your preoccupation with the lion must have distracted you from hearing the battle overhead with my adversaries tonight," Ra said. "We were not far away and I looked down and saw you were in trouble. I have managed to evade the others just for a short time, and used this chance to come down to assist you. You were kind to me when I needed help, and I wished to repay this when an opportunity presented itself."

"Thank you very much; you came just in time, otherwise my quest would have ended here and so would the lives of my friends," I added. "May I ask if you've observed anything yet on your daily travels that could help us?"

"It is little more than a day since you explained your mission to me, and I have not seen or heard anything since then," Ra replied. "But I shall remain alert to your needs. I must be on my way now before my foes discover where I am. Farewell; I am sure we shall meet again." With that, our friendly god sped away from us and was quickly out of sight.

Bebi volunteered to keep watch until daylight. Even though we were confident our visiting lion would not return, its colleagues would not have shared its experience with Ra and would have had no reservations about paying us a visit. I took my place on the grass with the others and we all tried to sleep. In the distance we could hear that the gods had resumed their nightly battle.

Chapter 4

Island Hopping

Once again Ra must have defeated his opponents, as we were awakened by his golden orb starting its journey across the heavens. Now that the danger of last night was behind us, our hunger pangs reminded us that we had not eaten since midday yesterday. Although this island was mainly concerned with animals, all of them contained at least some fruit-bearing trees. As we commenced our journey it did not take us long to gather some dates, figs and grapes. These would have to sustain us until we could find something more substantial.

As before, our two male companions led the way with Khumit and I following on behind. "Last night I thought our mission was about to be ended with us being torn to pieces by that lion," my attractive consort said. "I was really frightened for the second night in a row."

"I agree that it was certainly dangerous for a

time," I concurred. "It's fortunate for us that Ra came to help us just when he did, but it's also a coincidence that we've seen him two nights in a row. In both cases he brought calm to a troubled situation."

Khumit gave my arm a squeeze. "Yes it is, now that you mention it. I wonder if he's been appointed to watch over us, and will appear again if we run into more trouble."

"It might be, but he is the Supreme God. Who could have been in a position to issue him with such an instruction?"

"Maybe there are things we do not yet understand, and there is indeed someone who is superior to the gods, including Ra himself," she replied. With this thought in mind we walked on in silence.

An hour later we stopped for a brief rest. "When we met the fence repairers yesterday they said the coast was half a day's journey away," Bebi said. "Surely we must be close to it by now."

"Just let me go up this hill a little way to see if I can spot anything," I replied. As soon as I was a little higher up I could see the coastline not far ahead, and even the little boats tied up for travellers to use. I shouted down to my companions: "Yes, we only have a little further to go before we reach the sea. I can also see several houses in the distance, but there's also a farm near the road just ahead of us."

"We must call and see if there is someone who can let us have some food," Bebi said once I had rejoined the group. "Up to now we've seen few people on this island and it would be a good opportunity to speak with the farmers if they are there." Revived by the knowledge that we didn't have far to go we pressed on at a good pace and soon reached the farm building.

There were two worker shabti men in the yard cleaning their equipment. "Greetings my friends," Bebi said. "We are visitors to your island and have eaten all the food we have brought with us. Do you have some we can buy from you?"

"You are welcome here; we do not see many strangers on Animal Island, but you are the second party to pass this way in the last week" one of the farmers replied, smiling warmly. "Please come inside and we shall be happy to share some of our food with you."

We followed him into the house and sat down at a table whilst the other man went into the kitchen to prepare something to eat. He soon returned and set before us some bread, cheese, and eggs. As was the case with the previous farmer, there was a mug of home brewed beer for each of us. "This is extremely generous of you, good people," I said as we enthusiastically availed ourselves of the offerings. "We must pay you well for this."

"There will be no need for payment," the first farmer said. "But we would appreciate some help this afternoon as our two lady companions have gone over to Lake Island to collect some fish."

"We'd be glad to repay your kindness with some work," I replied, seeing the nods of agreement from my colleagues who were hungrily devouring the food. "But you said we're the second group of strangers to visit you recently. We heard from another farmer that they'd also been visited by men asking questions. I wonder if these are the same ones who visited you."

The farmer took a drink from his beer mug. "It sounds like those you speak of were indeed the same ones who questioned us. There were three men and they were not shabtis like us, but had been resurrected from their tombs. They told us they were the Senior Officials from Lake Island, and they asked if we knew the whereabouts of a man called Joseph."

As our hosts had already been questioned on the same matter that we were investigating, this time it would be easier for us to state the nature of our quest without trying to be devious. "That is an amazing coincidence," I said with just a hint of exaggeration. "We're also interested in this person, but not for the same reason as were your other visitors."

"How interesting," the farmer commented. "Can you tell us more?"

"We believe the three men who visited you had a grievance with Joseph that originated in their earthly life. They were jealous of his position in the Pharaoh's court but couldn't take their revenge then. But they are intent on destroying him here in the afterlife."

"That is barbaric; we are privileged to live in this paradise and should do so in peace and harmony with everyone, both shabtis and resurrected ones," the farmer said. "If Osiris comes to hear about this they will swiftly disappear from here and be reduced to dust."

"Indeed you are correct," I replied. "They should have left their grievances behind them, but this does not seem to be the case."

The farmer nodded. "You said a moment ago that your interest in this man was for a different reason. Can you explain?"

"I set off from Arable Island three days ago at the bidding of my master, Pharaoh Senusret the Third. He wished me to explore this Field of Reeds and seek out any signs of trouble or rebellion. Being a warrior in his earthly life had left him with the urge to take action to quell such incidents, should I discover any."

"Did he specifically mention this Joseph?"

"No, he had no knowledge of him, or at least of any trouble involving him. It was my colleagues Bebi, Intef and Khumit who first told me. We met by chance when they were visiting my island to gather food to take back to the Queen whom they served. They live on Flower Island, and very kindly accommodated me for the first night, and then decided to accompany me but only for two weeks."

"Do your friends here know of the three men who have been asking questions about Joseph's whereabouts?" the farmer asked, turning to face the others.

It was Bebi who answered. "No, we'd just heard rumours that some people had a grievance against him. It was only when the first farmer we met on your island told us about the same visit that you have had that we learned this. They even told him their names."

"Would you like to reveal them to us?"

"Indeed. They were Hepzefa, Neferu and Simontu. They had been senior members of their Pharaoh's court," Bebi replied.

Just like the activities of these three men were becoming common knowledge, I was again concerned that so was my quest. I had now revealed the truth to several others. Those whom I had met readily shared with me what they knew, and there was no doubt they would, with equal readiness, also tell others about what my colleagues and I were seeking. But if those who were planning to take their revenge on Joseph hear that I'm asking similar questions, I might be the first to feel their wrath. Caution was clearly needed from now on.

"If you've finished your meal," the farmer said, "we need to complete our work before the afternoon is over. Are you still prepared to assist us until our companions return with the fish?"

Bebi answered on behalf of all of us. "Of course we will, you have been so kind in feeding us and we shabtis are always ready to help each other. What do you wish us to do?"

"We need to take the ox cart into the fields, gather in the hay and then store it in the barn for our animals to feed on," he replied. "It's a lot work for just the two of us and we would be very grateful for your help so that we can complete this before nightfall."

Although we were glad to help the farmers, it would be growing dark by the time we had finished and once again there would be the matter of where to stay safely during the night. We would not relish a repeat of what happened when we camped in the open fields. But this would have to wait for now whilst we busied ourselves with the haymaking.

At last the job was done, and our farmer friends seemed happy to have a barn full of hay.

Their two female companions returned with their fish just as Ra had almost completed his journey for the day. "I'm sorry this job has taken so long," one of the farmers said, once we were all back inside the house armed with yet another mug of beer. "It would be too dangerous for you to continue your journey today, so you would be welcome to stay the night with us here in safety."

It didn't take us more than a few seconds to agree to this invitation, and we were glad not to have to prepare ourselves for another night in the open. "Good, then it's agreed," the farmer said. "Just rest now whilst we prepare some of this fish for our evening meal."

This must surely have been one of the best meals we had eaten enjoyed for a long time, with its generous portions of fresh fish and vegetables and yet more beer. Once it was over we sat back in the comfortable chairs to chat about the events of the day and our plans for tomorrow. However, the flickering light from a pair of oil lamps made it difficult to keep our eyes from closing so we agreed it was time for some well-earned sleep.

"You four can stay here in our living room if you wish, and we shall retire to our own bed chambers, one of the farmers said. "There'll be no danger for you tonight in here whatever happens outside." We expressed our gratitude and made ourselves comfortable, some deciding to sleep in the chairs whilst others preferred to stretch out on the floor. Whether or not the warring gods passed this way during the night we didn't know, because we only awakened when the welcoming sunlight was trying to find its way through the gaps in the window shutters.

"I hope you had a restful night," the first farmer said as he entered the room. "I'm sure you'd like to break your fast with some food before you continue your journey. We shall also pack something to sustain you during the day."

"Once again you are being most kind," Bebi answered. "Whilst we dine together, can you please tell us if you've heard anything about this man, Joseph, that might help us in our quest?"

The farmer gave a knowing smile "As you probably guessed, in a rural community like this there are few secrets. We've met other farmers yes, and there's been talk of him, as there will also be about your own presence here."

"It does concern us that what started out as a secret mission for us is now out in the open," I said. "My main concern is that if – or should I say when – it reaches the three men, we may find ourselves being silenced even before they find

Joseph."

"Indeed you might be in trouble, so it's important you reach your goal before they do," the farmer replied. "But to return to your question on what we know of this matter, the men who are seeking him in revenge said they lived on Lake Island which is next to ours. This must mean that Joseph is not permanently located there otherwise they would've found him already. You will know there are many islands in this Field of Reeds and it will take you a long time to explore them all."

"Yes, this is a concern, at least for my three companions. They only have two weeks before they must be back serving their Queen, and we are already into the fourth day. It's most likely Joseph is aware he is being sought for nefarious purposes, and is therefore continually moving around to evade discovery."

"That's indeed a valid point," said the farmer. "There's little I can say that will be useful, except perhaps one thing. With the speed that knowledge of your own search to protect him will be circulating, he might be tempted to deliberately seek you out."

"So maybe the fact that word travels fast in this land can be used to our advantage rather than against us," Bebi commented. "This takes away some of our concern that our mission is no longer a secret. Perhaps we should now be quite open about it to everyone we meet."

"I'm pleased you now have at least something to guide you," our farmer said. "You'll have seen that many of the houses on Animal Island are clustered nearby so, before you decide to cross the water again, you might wish to walk over to them and speak to some of my neighbours."

With that we thanked our farmer friends for looking after us so well, and set off with renewed confidence to visit the other houses. "The more I think about it, the more I like the idea of us being open about our intention," Bebi commented. "Do you think we should go so far as saying that your master, Pharaoh Senusret, wishes to use his powers to suppress anything that could disturb the peace of this land?"

"That would certainly be close to the truth," I replied. "The Pharaoh didn't give me any specific guidelines, but just said he wanted to know if there was any trouble that would give him the excuse to mount an attack and suppress it. I don't have time to go back now and ask him, so I shall take it upon myself to make the decisions. We might even go as far as to say that my master would welcome Joseph into his court and offer him protection."

"Yes, that could mean that Joseph might come to hear about this even before we find him.

If so, he could decide to go straight to Arable Island and seek sanctuary there."

"It would certainly save us the trouble of escorting him there ourselves, especially if the three men tried to stop us," I said as we were approaching the first of the houses.

During the morning we spoke with many of the shabti farmers who were working in their homes or fields, and each of the conversations followed a similar pattern: "Did you know of Joseph and where he might be?" We would then be told that three men had been asking the same question, and why did we want to know. Our response would be: "Pharaoh Senusret on Arable Island has heard that he might be in trouble and wishes to protect him." The exchanges would end with our request to let Joseph know this if they ever came across him.

It was now mid day and we had completed all we could accomplish here. We sat down and enjoyed the food our hosts had packed for us and discussed what to do next. "Shall we row across to Lake Island and continue there what we have just been doing here?" Bebi asked.

"Now that we seem to have a successful strategy, yes, we can go there now and see how many people we can meet there before we have to seek somewhere for the night," I replied. "However, there's something we need to remember: the three men told those who have met them that they lived on that island. Are we risking being confronted by them if we visit their domain?"

Bebi considered this for a few moments before saying anything. "Yes, that's something we need to consider," he eventually replied. "But hopefully they'll still be on their tour of neighbouring islands, just as we are. We're probably safe in assuming they'll be away, and it may be a good opportunity to go there now before they return."

Intef and Khumit agreed so, once we had completed our meal, we walked toward where the boats were tied up. An hour later we landed on Lake Island and made our way inland to look for residents to talk with.

What a contrast this was to the other islands we'd visited, and especially the last one. Instead of it comprising fields for the animals and a small number of farm houses, as its name befits there were lakes and ponds as far as we could see. These were fed by streams that must have had their source below a mountain we could just make out in the distance. On some of the lakes fishermen were at work in small boats whilst others sat by the waterside using rod and net. Several lodges had been erected for the workers to protect them from the elements and in case they were unable to return home before dark.

Engaging with the local people this time seemed almost too easy after our struggles over the last few days when we had tried to avoid revealing the true purpose of our mission. During the afternoon we chatted to more than twenty shabtis who were busy with their fishing. Yes, they did know that Hepzefa, Nefferu and Simontu lived on Lake Island in palatial residences somewhere near the central mountain. But these three rarely ventured further afield, preferring to send their servants out to procure the local fish as well as foods from other islands. It was thus a surprise to find them knocking on doors and asking questions.

The fishermen suspected that the trio wanted to find Joseph to do him harm, and all responded they had no idea where their unfortunate victim could be found, even if they actually knew. We explained that my Pharaoh was willing to defend Joseph against those seeking their revenge, and thus take away the need for him to be constantly on the move to avoid capture.

However, as with others we had questioned, they were initially guarded in revealing what they knew. Once they had confidence we were telling the truth, several of them confided in us that Joseph had also been here seeking a place to hide. When he'd heard that his antagonists were trying to find him, he swiftly departed saying he'd have to keep travelling to avoid capture. We then we asked the fishermen if they knew where he'd go to next, and their reply was always that they didn't know.

Although we had received helpful information from our questioning, we were now becoming increasingly concerned that we were exposing ourselves to the risk of attack by these three men who were intent on taking their revenge on Joseph. They would no doubt ruthlessly deal with anyone who stood in their way, including us. Perhaps we should leave this island as soon as we could without exploring its length and breadth, but the afternoon was nearing its end and we would first have to find somewhere to shelter.

"Why not ask one of the fishermen who has a lodge near the lake if we could use it, just for the one night?" Khumit suggested.

"Good idea," I agreed. "Let's go and speak with just one more resident. If he seems friendly and is not intending to camp there himself, maybe he'll let us do so."

"Of course you may stay the night in my cabin," a very jolly fisherman said. "I'm always happy to help out fellow shabtis. You'll find it rather cramped for the four of you, but nobody should still be outside when the gods start their usual nonsense."

"That's very kind of my friend. How can we compensate you for this?" Bebi asked.

"No need to do so, although the place could benefit from a good clean because I've neglected to do so for ages. I shall leave you some of my fish to eat. If you build a fire outside now you should be able to cook them before it gets dark, and then shut yourselves safely inside the lodge for the night."

We thanked our kind fisherman as he packed up his equipment and departed for home. Whilst Intef and I collected some wood to build the fire, Bebi and Khumit busied themselves cleaning and tidying the cabin, making space on the floor for the four of us to lie down as they did so. An hour later, after a very welcome hot meal, we locked ourselves in the building. But before trying to sleep, we reviewed what we'd achieved so far, and what our strategy should now be.

As this was my mission, I thought it best to speak first. "This is the fourth island I've been on in less than a week, and so far there's been no sign of this man Joseph. Of course I was not looking for him in my own domain on Arable Island before I left but, had he been there seeking refuge, it's certain I would have heard about it. We won't have the time to visit all the many islands in this Field of Reeds together because the three of you will soon have to return to your home. I don't relish the thought of continuing all on my own."

"I agree we can't visit all the islands," Bebi said. "Even if we did there's no certainty we'd ever find him. Those three men will have been looking much longer than we have and they've not yet succeeded."

"Pharaoh Senusret would me most unhappy if I were to return to him admitting I'd failed to discover any trouble that he could enjoy putting down. At least he'd demote me and perhaps even make sure I was shut away somewhere. He is not a forgiving man. We need to take a new approach to this quest."

"Have you any ideas?" Khumit asked. "I cannot bear to think of you being locked up so I shall never be able to see you again."

"It's so kind of you to say this," I replied, feeling just a little embarrassed that was not helped by the laughs coming from the two men. "But the answer would be to encourage Joseph to come to Arable Island itself. He's probably been running from one island to another for some time now and it's likely he'll eventually arrive there anyway. If he hears he may obtain protection there he may wish to meet us as soon as he can."

Intef was not a man who said very much, preferring action to words, but he now spoke up.

"I like your plan, Metjen, and I'm sure he'll do as you say once he has word he'll be welcome on your island. But remember that the three men who are plotting vengeance on him will quickly follow. There'll no longer be any secrets, and your Pharaoh will no doubt then have the chance to satisfy his urge to engage in some physical combat."

"I agree with what's been said, and it seems we now have a plan," Bebi commented. "But we still have a week before those of us from Flower Island need to report back there for duty. I suggest we retrace our steps and spend another day on each of the islands as we go. We can explore parts we did not visit before and question more people; we just might pick up some new clues. You, Metjen, will then have to return to Arable Island and continue the quest on your own."

"Let's hope I'll have something useful to report to my master," I said. "But we should rest now whilst we can, safe in this little cabin; our experience two nights ago reminded us that we might not always be so fortunate as to be offered such protection."

We laid down and did our best to sleep, despite the noise coming from outside. But this time it was not caused by the warring gods but by the heavy rain beating down like a drum onto the wooden roof. Whilst the other islands benefit from periodic gentle showers to nourish the plant life, the many streams and lakes on this one needed frequent replenishment from the heavens.

* * *

The rain had stopped and the sun was shining by the time we were wakened by the sound of someone knocking on the cabin door. It was the fisherman returning to continue his daily routine. "Sorry we were not already up and ready to leave by this time," I said apologetically. "But we much appreciate your kindness in letting us use your accommodation for the night."

"Oh it's my pleasure, and there's no need to apologise," he replied. "It's the custom of those in my trade to make an early start if we're to catch our daily quota of fish. And I've also brought some food to sustain you as you travel on," he added, unpacking some bread, cheese and fruit.

We had been helped so much during the last few days that it was becoming difficult to find adequate words to express our thanks. Leaving our latest benefactor in peace to commence his work, we took the food with us to eat a little later rather than delay him by remaining any longer. Our plan was to visit some more parts of this island during the morning, and then row back to Animal Island to do the same there in the afternoon.

"If we circle to our left, we shall not be retracing our steps back to the coast," Intef suggested. What we saw was much the same as on our inward journey yesterday, with solitary or small groups of fishermen sitting by a lake or sailing on it busy with their catch.

When we stopped to eat our food Bebi looked into the distance. "The fishermen rarely stay in their little cabins at night, so their houses must be further inland. "We're not learning anything new today by just talking to individuals who are at the lakes, so perhaps we should visit some of their homes before we take our leave."

As no one dissented, once we'd finished eating we took a path toward the central peak. Sure enough we soon came in sight of some houses well clear of the water, safe from any flooding that might occur. Seeing some female shabtis together outside the nearest dwelling, we approached them. When they saw us walking toward them it was clear they were wary of strangers, and were ready to quickly retreat into their houses if necessary.

"Greetings my fellow shabtis," I said in as friendly a voice as I could muster. "Please do not be concerned. We are visitors from other islands exploring your bit of paradise and will soon be on our way again." As this seemed to result in a relaxing of any initial anxiety, I continued by following with our current strategy of coming straight to the point. "We've chatted to some of your men folk who are fishing on the lakes, and one of them was kind enough to let us stay the night in his cabin."

"Ah, so you are the strangers we've heard about," one of the women said. Pointing to the shabti on her right she continued, "My friend's partner is the one who gave you shelter, and he has told us about your mission."

This at least saved us from the effort of having to explain everything from the start. "We are very grateful to your man," I said, bowing toward the female in question. "You'll therefore know that we are seeking information on the whereabouts of Joseph and the three men who are wishing to do him harm. Do any of you know anything that might help us?"

"You'll have been told that we've all been visited both by the three men and later Joseph himself," the first shabti responded. "It's likely they've all left Lake Island by now, although we don't know where they'll have gone to next. But if the three men don't succeed in their quest soon, it's certain they'll want to return to their palatial homes here. Being deprived of the luxuries they've been used to will not have pleased them."

"That's interesting," Bebi interjected. "But if they fail this time I suspect they'll just try again later – or perhaps send their servants out to find Joseph for them. Either way, it's important we get to him first and offer him protection so as to take away the threat on his life once and for all."

The shabtis all seemed pleased to hear this. "We know Joseph to be a virtuous man who did only good in his earthly existence. I'm sure we'd all be happy to know he'll be permanently safe from these evil resurrected ones, their spokesperson commented."

"It's good to know that we're all of the same mind," I said. "We'd better be on our way now and continue our search here before moving to another island."

Chapter 5

Encounter with the Enemy

We bade our farewells and continued inland along the same path. "I'm wondering if we'll gain anything by continuing to question the locals here," said Bebi. "We must leave ourselves sufficient time to row back to Animal Island and find somewhere to shelter before nightfall."

"Yes, perhaps we've learned all we can from this island, and we know that neither Joseph nor the three men are here now," I agreed. "What do you think Intef and Khumit?"

"We certainly don't want to spend another night out of doors, after our last experience," Khumit replied.

"I agree," said Intef. "But I see that just ahead of us the path divides. If we take the one to the left we should circle back to the coast where the boats are and arrive there shortly after the sun has reached its zenith."

We made our way past one lake after

another, many with fishermen in attendance. Instead of stopping to chat, we just waved to them and continued on our journey. After about two hours we made a brief stop to rest. "The sun is already high but I cannot see the coast yet," I said. "Perhaps we should ask the next person we see how far we still have to travel." A short distance further on we saw one of the locals sitting by a lake and went to speak with him.

"But this path doesn't lead directly to the sea," he said. "You are still walking across the island. If you continue just a little further you'll come to a crossroad. Turn left and then stay on it until you reach the coast."

"And how long will still take?"

"If you manage to keep going, you should be there in about three hours."

We thanked him and then walked on, trying to maintain a brisk pace. But we had already lost some of our energy due to our morning's exertion. Bebi tried to sound positive: "If we keep going like this we shall still have time to row across the water before it is dark. I'm sure there will be some accommodation for us there where we can spend the night."

Although it was still daylight, the afternoon was nearly over by the time we did eventually reach our destination. "I'll go and prepare the boat for us," Intef said, as the other three of us sat on the grass for a few minutes to rest our weary legs. We also became aware that we had not eaten anything since the pack of food our friendly fisherman had given us as we let his cabin.

Intef quickly came running back to us in an agitated state. "Metjen, Bebi, Khumit, there are only two boats and they've both been wrecked. I suspect they were dashed onto the rocks by the fierce storm we had last night. We can't leave here until someone rows over from the other island and lets us have their boat."

"What are we to do if nobody comes across here soon?" Khumit said in an agitated voice. "We didn't pass any houses or lodges in the last hour, and there will not be time to walk further inland to find one before it's dark."

"Can we use what's left of the boats to assemble some sort of shelter if we are unable to leave here before nightfall?" I asked Intef. "We did manage to do so the last time we had to remain outdoors."

"I can try, and it would help if we had some branches from the trees to use as well," he replied.

"Whilst I go and help Intef, you try to break off some of the branches," Bebi said to me. "Perhaps Khumit could go with you and see if there are any fruits or nuts on the trees ready for harvesting. I shall also keep looking to see if any boats are coming this way, and call you if there are."

We all went about our tasks without delay, mindful of the dangers at night if we were out in the open and the gods chose this location to play their war games. After half an hour of using all my strength, I managed to strip several branches from the trees and drag them toward the beach. Intef and Bebi were already on the shoreline trying to position loose planks and other wreckage from the boats next to the trunk of a thick tree.

"Ah, those will be helpful," Intef exclaimed when he saw what I had brought. "I have some strips of wood that'll form part of a roof but the leafy branches will fill in the gaps. They will also provide camouflage against any dangers that pass above us. Three us should be able to squeeze into the space beneath whilst one remains outside on guard, as we did when we had to camp outside on Animal Island."

Khumit arrived carrying some figs, grapes and dates in her pulled up skirt. "I managed to find something to eat," she said, looking rather apprehensively at the makeshift shelter that was taking shape. "Is there any sign of boats coming so we don't have to use this primitive shelter? I'm still fearful of what happened to us before."

Bebi looked across the expanse of water

separating us from the next island. "Sorry, nothing is happening. Even if someone sets off now it'll be too dark for us to row back by the time they arrive here. I'm afraid we shall just have to make the best of things and camp here for the night. At least there will be no lions here to disturb us this time."

We finished our makeshift shelter and, in the fading light, sat down to enjoy the food that Khumit had gathered. "I volunteer for the first shift this time," Bebi said. "Then perhaps you, Metjen and finally Intef." There were no dissenters, so three of us crawled inside the structure and tried to sleep.

Khumit was facing me. "I'm glad you are here with me," she whispered, touching my hand. "When we set off on this journey I didn't think we'd be faced with having to spend nights outside like this. There are dangers both from the heavens and the land, and I can't stop myself feeling worried about our safety."

I gave her hand a squeeze and said softly, "This is paradise and we shall be protected. It was so kind of the three of you to accompany me on this mission, and I could not have achieved all we have done on my own. Let's try to sleep now and give our bodies a chance to recover from the physical exertion of today. It'll be my turn next to go outside to be on guard."

Bebi gently shook me awake. It felt as if I'd only been asleep for a few minutes but it was nearly three hours. "It's all been quiet and peaceful outside, with no sound of the gods up to their tricks," he reported, taking my place in the shelter." I just hoped it would be the same for me, I thought as I sat down on a nearby sand dune.

A waning, yellow moon and the glittering stars above provided just enough light for me to see the waves gently rolling onto the beach. I was sure the sea was closer to us now than it was when we arrived, so tidal forces must be at work. Because our camp was just off the beach it would be above the waterline, so we shouldn't have to worry about being flooded. The sound of the regular ebbing and flowing of the water was starting to have a hypnotic effect on me and it required all my effort to stay awake, especially after just being roused from my slumbers.

Maybe I must have dozed off for a few minutes because I was suddenly alerted by a different sound. It was as if something was swishing the sand from side to side. I scanned the beach but the moon was now starting to disappear below the horizon and it provided little light. The noise was growing louder and a grunting sound had now been added to it. I stood up, intending to search around the campsite, and saw it just in time.

The open jaws of a large crocodile snapped shut just inches from where my leg had been a moment earlier. Jumping out of the creature's way I frantically looked for a weapon, and grabbed a piece of timber that had not been used for our shelter. Using it to beat the animal on the nose, I tried to entice it away from the camp by moving down the beach whilst continuing my attack. Fortunately it waddled after me but I managed to evade its repeated attempts to take hold of me.

Although I hadn't called out to those in the shelter, the sound of commotion quickly alerted them. They immediately emerged, found pieces of discarded wood or tree branches and joined me in my attempt to get rid of this unwelcome visitor.

It proved to be no match for the crocodile against the four of us, especially when Intef managed to wedge a piece of planking into its mouth. We were very relieved when it obviously realised it wasn't going to have us for its next meal, and made its way back into the sea as fast as its stubby legs and swishing tale would allow.

"Thank you so much for your prompt help," I said whilst trying to get my breath back. "I didn't realise these dangerous animals were in the sea here, otherwise we could have made a point of looking out for them."

"Now that we've had this experience for ourselves, I do recall being told to watch out for these saltwater crocodiles by those who go out on the sea to fish," Bebi commented. "Sorry I forgot about this otherwise I'd have mentioned this when we set up camp."

"I'll take over the watch now," Intef announced. "The rest of you can go back inside and complete your slumbers. Be assured that I shall keep a close look out in case our aquatic friend or any of its colleagues try to bother us again."

We were grateful to him for taking over earlier than he needed to, but we lay down to try and sleep again knowing that we were in safe hands.

* * *

"Come on, wake up you lazy lot. I think there may be a boat that's just set off from Animal Island." It was Intef, bright and cheerful as the sun that was just appearing over the horizon. We crawled out of our makeshift shelter rubbing the sleep from our eyes, and looked over to where he was pointing.

"Yes, you're right, and I can see that the oars are moving," said Bebi. "We should be able to leave this place in an hour." Turning to Khumit he asked, "Is there any food left?" She brought several pieces of fruit from a small pile next to the shelter and we sat down to enjoy them, feeling much more cheerful than we did last night.

As the boat drew nearer we could see it contained three men, and were able to tell from the amount of splashing that they were clearly not very skilled at synchronised rowing. We went down the beach to meet them and it was obvious from their attire they were not worker shabtis like us but noblemen resurrected from their tombs. "Greetings, my lords," Bebi said respectfully. "We're very pleased you have rowed over to this island because we are unable to leave without a boat. Unfortunately, those that were moored here were wrecked by a storm."

The men looked at us disdainfully, and one said, "I suppose you shabtis will be able to use this one now, but what if we then need a boat ourselves once you take it away?"

"As soon as we arrive on Animal Island I shall tell those responsible for maintaining these craft that some new ones are required here. They'll be able to bring some over for you straight away," replied Bebi.

"Very well then, but you better be right if you want to avoid our wrath," the nobleman said. "Why do you want to leave in such a hurry – are you running away from something?"

What unpleasant people these three are turning out to be, I thought. But we needed to remain calm and avoid angering them. "Sir, I'm Metjen and my home is on Arable Island. My three friends are from Flower Island, and we have been exploring other parts of this Field of Reeds. We now wish to return to our homes."

"Well I am Hepzefa and those with me are Neferu and Simontu. We live here on Lake Island in our palace near the central peak."

Perhaps we should have suspected who this trio might be, especially as we'd been told earlier they would return to their homes for a time if they hadn't found their quarry. Whilst their arrival here indicated they'd not found Joseph, it still came as a shock to find we were now being unexpectedly confronted by them. We needed to be careful not to disclose our own mission. However, we had intentionally made no secret of it to those we had spoken with over the last two days. Had these vindictive men already heard about us?

Hepzefa spoke again. "You, Metjen, say you live on Arable Island, and so does Pharaoh Senusret. Do you know him?"

If I lied to them now I would no doubt be caught out later and would be in trouble. "Yes sir, in fact he recently appointed me as his Vizier."

"So, he must have sent you out on this journey you refer to as an exploration. There would have been a purpose behind it. What was it?"

"My Pharaoh wishes to know more about the islands he has not yet personally visited. I'm to report back to him with my recommendations so he can plan a grand tour of those which might be of most interest to him."

That was close enough to the truth to avoid the need for me to lie only to be caught out later, I thought. Would this satisfy my questioner? "We know Senusret to be a man who enjoys action, so there must be some motivation behind this," he said. Do you know what it is, shabti?"

"Sir, he did not give me any reason, except that he was bored and wanted some adventure."

It seemed that Hepzefa was satisfied with this, at least for the present. "We knew his father, and were members of his court at the time he appointed a man called Joseph to run the country for him. Tell me, did your master ever speak of this Joseph?"

I could answer this truthfully, because it was only when I met my three friends that I was told about him. "No sir, I've never heard him mention this man."

"Very well. But we would like to meet Joseph ourselves again to reminisce about the times we were together. If you should see him on your travels you must come back to this island and inform us where he is. Do not tell him about us, as we would like to make it a surprise visit."

"We shall do as you request, sir," I replied, trying to make this sound convincing.

"If we find out that you have deceived us, you will all be in trouble. Do you understand?" Hepzefa said with a menacing tone of voice. We gave him our assurances with as much deference as we could muster, doing our best to hide our growing contempt for this unpleasant man.

It was important these three individuals did nothing to prevent us taking the only available boat so that we could leave this island. They must have accepted our story as, with no final pleasantries, they turned away from us and made their way inland.

Once they were out of sight as well as earshot, we chatted about the amazing coincidence that had brought us in contact with this vengeful trio. We also hoped they'd fully accepted our story, although there was no doubt they would retaliate if they discovered the truth. But it was time to board our boat and row across the water to Animal Island before anything else prevented us.

An hour later we tied up at the small jetty, pleased to see that the presence of other boats indicated they had not suffered the same fate as had those at the island we had camped on last night. "Maybe the storm was just centred on Lake Island, due to its central peak and the need for plenty of rain to maintain the water levels," surmised Bebi.

My first task was to find those responsible for supplying and maintaining the boats and ask them to take some over to replace those that were destroyed.

"Now that we're here, what are our plans – we've already explored Animal Island?" asked Intef.

"Yes, I suppose we could have rowed right around it and not bothered to land," Bebi replied. "But it's a big island and we might as well see if there have been any developments since we were last here."

"Yes, and we can take a different path this time, although we must make sure we've somewhere inside to stay after our earlier encounters with the lion and crocodile," I said. The four of us started walking in the opposite direction to the cluster of homes we had called at during our previous visit.

Once we had left the small settlement, just as we experienced last time there were long distances between the farm houses. We stopped at some of them, and also spoke with those we met working in the fields. Nobody was able to add to what we already knew. We'd suspected that the three men had recently visited to ask about Joseph, but the residents always replied that they didn't know where he was.

"We appear to be wasting our time again here," Bebi said. "Let's travel back along the path we used three days ago and see if we can reach the farmhouse we stayed at before. Shakir and Bennu were very kind and they may be able to help us again." This seemed a good idea, so we diverted to the right and eventually joined the route that bisected the island close to were we had the encounter with the lion.

"I still shudder at the memory of that night," Khumit said as we walked past the remains of our camp. "If it had not been for the intervention of Ra we wouldn't be here now."

"Well, I'm sure some of us would have survived," I replied, putting my arm around her shoulder. "Remember that Intef has a knife and he knows how to use it. But lions also hunt during the day so we may not be free of danger even now."

"I heard that," Intef said. "Yes, my knife is always ready, but it would be wise if we each had a strong stick in our hands just in case. By the way, we've not had a decent meal for ages and I'm hungry. Let's see if there's anything we can gather from the fields."

Half an hour later we continued on our journey, munching a few dates we had managed to find. Each of us was now armed with a stick sharpened at one end by Intef. As before we could see the occasional house in the distance but encountered few people on the road.

"I'm wondering if we're still not making the best use of the time we've left together on this mission," Bebi said after we had been walking for over an hour. "We're learning nothing and it's already afternoon. Perhaps we should have rowed right around this island after all."

"You might turn out to be right," I replied. "But we've no choice now but to continue on and hope our luck will improve before we're able to leave for Flower Island."

Intef had been walking in front of us, keeping a lookout for any sign of danger. He stopped and said, "I can see ahead two shabtis who appear to working on the fences, along with an ox cart, and I'm sure they are the same ones we met on our outward journey."

"Greetings again," one of them said as we reached their position. "We didn't expect to see you again so soon. Did you have a successful journey to wherever it was you were going?"

"Thank you, yes," Bebi replied. "But it could've been a disaster because we had to camp outside for the night after we left you, and were attacked by a lion."

"This doesn't surprise me; you don't want to be out in the open when Ra has completed his journey across the heavens and has then to defend himself against his enemies."

"Fortunately it was Ra himself who saved us, and the following night a farmer near the coast kindly provided shelter," Bebi continued.

"Where are you headed now?" the shabti asked.

"We're going to the coast to take a boat back to Flower Island," I said. "But we shall also call on the farmer we stayed with on our outward journey. We don't want to spend another night unprotected."

"We know most of the farmers on this island. What's his name?"

"It was Shakir and his female companion is Bennu. We helped them with the milking to repay them for their hospitality."

"Ah yes, I know them well and they're always willing to help travellers," he commented. "But you're not he only strangers who have passed this way recently. Only two days ago we were confronted by three of the resurrected ones, and they were not very friendly."

Bebi spoke up again. "We're sure we know who they were, as they also spoke to us as we were leaving Lake Island. Did they ask you any questions?"

"They said they were seeking a man called Joseph, and did we know where he was."

"Were you able to help them?"

"Although we had heard of him, we could truthfully answer that we had no knowledge of his whereabouts. They said we had to report to them if we learned later where he was, otherwise we would suffer for our silence."

"They gave us the same warning. Not very nice people, are they, said Bebi."

"But there's more," the workman said. "Only yesterday another stranger came along this road and stopped to talk with us. He said his name was Joseph."

On hearing this we all gasped in amazement. At last we would have the opportunity to question someone who had seen him such a short time ago. Perhaps Joseph might even still be on this island and we would not have wasted our time being here after all. "Did he tell you where he was going," I asked, trying not to sound too excited."

"Yes, he did but please first tell us what your interest is in him. He seemed to be a very decent man who had to be continually on the move to prevent something bad happening to him. We would like to help him rather than make his situation worse."

Once again, if we were going to learn anything useful it would be necessary to reveal the true purpose of our mission. "We're trying to find Joseph so that we can offer him the protection of my master, Pharaoh Senusret, who lives on Arable Island," I began. "He instructed me to tour this paradise to see if there was any rebellion or other troubles that needed to be suppressed."

"Indeed we've already heard of your Pharaoh and his reputation for action," the workman said. "Osiris would not usually welcome violence in this peaceful place but, if it's carried out to prevent evil, it would surely be acceptable to him."

"Can you now tell us where Joseph said he was going?" I asked.

"We suggested to him that he visit farmer Shakir just as you did. Joseph will have needed to stay the night somewhere as you will again. Maybe he'll still be at the farmhouse. If he's already left there, the farmer may know where he planned to go next."

"This is very helpful; thank you for confiding in us," I replied. "We were just saying amongst ourselves that we were wasting our time being on this island. But what you've just told us has made it worthwhile."

"Good luck in your mission; we don't want

to think that Joseph will have to keep running for ever. He deserves to enjoy the peace that was created for us here, and those who wish to do him harm should be banished." We bid the two workers farewell and continued on our journey with renewed enthusiasm. Would we soon succeed in our quest to find our man and offer him sanctuary?

"It would be wonderful if Joseph were still with the farmer," Khumit said to me. "You could then return to your master with him and your mission will be over."

"I'm not going to start celebrating just yet," I answered with a laugh. "Firstly he has to be there; secondly we shall have to convince him he will be safe under the protection of Senusret and, thirdly, we have to escort him there without those three evil men discovering what we are doing."

Khumit nodded in agreement. "Of course you're correct, and there is another thing I have been thinking about."

"Which is?"

"When all this is over, you will be on Arable Island and I shall be back on Flower Island serving my Queen. Despite the dangers we've already faced, I've enjoyed our adventures together. Life will become very dull for me."

I put my arm around her but didn't immediately reply. Perhaps similar thoughts were also going through my own mind. We walked on in silence, saving our breath for coping with the brisk pace we had adopted to reach our destination as soon as possible. As the afternoon was drawing to a close, the farm came into view. Tired and hungry we arrived at the gate and were pleased to see Shakir and Bennu in the yard busy with the second milking of the day.

Tut their dog saw us first and his barking caused the farmers to look up to see what had prompted his excitement. As soon as they saw us they got up from their stools and came to open the gate. "We didn't expect to see you so soon again, but you are welcome," Shakir said, smiling.

"Thank you," we each responded as we entered quickly so he could shut the gate before any animals waiting to be milked had the chance to escape.

"When we last met, you said you were on a mission for your Pharaoh to try and find something where he could enjoy being a military general again," the farmer said as we walked back to where he and Bennu had been working.

"Yes, and you told us about your meeting with Hepzefa, Nefferu and Simontu and how they were seeking Joseph," I replied. "They instructed you to let them know if you should discover where Joseph can be found."

"That's correct, but we had no intention of doing this."

I was impatient to know if Joseph had been to their farm. "Earlier today we met some men who were repairing the fences. They informed us that Joseph had passed by a couple of days ago, and they had suggested to him that he call on you, just as we are doing. Please do tell us if he did come, and if he's still here."

"Yes he was here two days ago. We fed him and sheltered him for the night in the same barn you stayed in. But no to your second question; he left yesterday to travel on, concerned that the three men might come back along this road and find him."

"A pity we missed him by just one day," I replied, disappointed. "Did he say where he was going to next?"

"You are still impatient, my friend Metjen, as I was about to tell you. He is weary of having to keep moving to evade capture, and longs to be where he can live peacefully without this constant fear of attack. We did inform him of your own mission, but he was a little wary of your master's true intention. He asked us if we thought he really would be safe there with the Pharaoh."

"And did you give him assurances that he would?"

"We could not do so because we did not

have the first-hand knowledge that you do. All we could say was what you told us the first time you visited us."

"Shakir, I do understand your position," I assured him. "Of course you can only pass on what you know. Also, you've put yourself at risk by defying the instruction to report Joseph's whereabouts to the three men."

"Please don't worry about that, Metjen. But we've been talking for too long and the milking has to be completed before it's dark. Perhaps you'd all like to help us again, and we can then provide a meal and shelter for you as we did last time."

Bebi decided he should answer on our behalf. "I'm sorry we've kept you from your work, and thank you so much for extending your hospitality to us once again. Of course we'll be glad to help, and also with the morning milking; it's the least we can do to repay your kindness. I just hope we shall be more skilful doing this than we were last time."

Although there were many things I still wanted to ask, Bebi was right and we owed it to our two farmer friends to give them all the help they needed. We completed the milking just as Ra had reached the end of his journey across the heavens, and then retired for a most welcome meal in the comfort of the farmhouse.

When we were relaxing afterwards I took the opportunity to ask some more questions about Joseph. "Thank you once again for the food, Shakir and Bennu. We've been surviving mostly on the fruit we could gather as we travelled. You said earlier that Joseph had some doubts about how genuine my Pharaoh's offer of protection might be, but did he say he would go to my home island anyway?"

"No, he just said that he would have to keep moving to avoid capture. But by tomorrow when you depart he will only be two days ahead of you. This means he will either be on this island or will have already rowed across to Flower Island. I'm sure you'll catch up with him before long."

"We hope so, and at least the options of where Joseph will be are much narrower now than they were when we first embarked on this quest," I said, patting Tut who had come to sit by my side. "But it would be most helpful if you can tell us what he looked like so we can recognise him if our paths do cross."

"Of course," Shakir replied. "Joseph was an old man of more than one hundred years when he died, but he remains an imposing figure and is taller than me. His hair, moustache and neatly trimmed beard are all grey by now as you might expect. He was wearing a brown tunic that reached to his ankles, and had a dark blue cloak to wrap around him when it's cold. In his hands he carried a long staff to aid his walking; on the top of it there were carvings of two flowers."

"This is all very useful," Bebi said. "I'm sure he will be easy to distinguish from the local people. But we're keeping you both from your rest. If there's nothing more to add, did you say we can sleep in your barn again tonight?"

"Of course you are most welcome to do so," Shakir said. "I just hope you don't have a repeat of the disturbance you had last time." Exhausted after such a tiring day, we walked over to the barn, made up some bedding with straw and the blankets we'd been given and lay down to sleep. Although we occasionally heard distant sounds of the gods enjoying their nightly battle, we were not troubled by them and enjoyed a restful night.

Chapter 6

The Net Closes

We arose as soon as Ra began to light up the land, remembering we'd agreed to assist with the morning milking before leaving. Shakir and Bennu insisted on sharing their food with us again before any work was done, and we then did our best to help with the work. Once we had finished we bade our farming friends farewell and set off along the coastal path.

"It's important we reach the boats and row across to Flower Island without delay so that we'll have sufficient time to find shelter before dark," Bebi said. "It took us two hours of brisk walking to reach Shakir and Bennu's farm on our journey here. Perhaps we can complete the outward one more quickly if we have fewer stops."

"We can try," Khumit agreed, "But yesterday was exhausting and I still haven't fully recovered from the exertion, plus the milking we did this morning. Perhaps the rest of you should go on ahead of me if I'm too slow; I can always catch up with you later."

This should not have come as a surprise to us. We had each been pushing ourselves to the limit with little consideration for our health and strength, spurred on by the thought that our quest would soon achieve its goal. There had been danger, and on some days there had been little food to sustain us, but we hadn't let this slow us down. Now all this neglect of what it was doing to our bodies was making itself known to us. We needed to discuss this before we went one step further.

As it was my mission I felt guilty for what I was doing to my friends. "You are right to bring this up Khumit, and I sincerely apologise to each of you for selfishly ignoring your welfare. It was so kind of you all to volunteer to help me when there was no obligation to do so. I was very grateful when you did, and am now so sorry for what I've been putting you through."

"There's no need to apologise, Metjen, we came willingly for the adventure and because of the camaraderie we shabtis share," Bebi said. "Although at first we were unsure of your Pharaoh's true motive, we would like to see Joseph safe and those three evil men receive the punishment from Osiris they deserve."

"Thank you for saying this, my friend," I

replied. "But we still need to decide what to do now. I refuse to leave Khumit behind to bravely continue on her own and would rather abandon the mission than let this happen."

Khumit came close and put her arm around my waist. "Thank you Metjen," was all she could manage to say whilst trying to keep her voice steady.

"I have an idea," said Intef. "We could split into two groups. I still feel I can press on at a good pace. If Bebi feels the same way, the two of us can go ahead and see if we can learn anything about Joseph. We can also make sure there'll be a boat for us. Metjen and Khumit will follow as best they can, and we'll then all meet at the landing stage."

"It's a good suggestion," Bebi commented. "But, if we separate, we shall be more vulnerable if we encounter a wild animal or other danger. Should we just stay together and make the best progress we can?"

"I'm sure we shall be alright in pairs, and I don't want to be responsible for jeopardising this mission," said Khumit. "If Metjen is willing, it would be sensible to split up as Intef suggests. We each still have our pointed stick to defend ourselves, should we need them."

Everyone looked at me for a decision. "If the rest of you are prepared to do this, then I agree.

I'm sure we can all look after ourselves, and it would speed things up if Intef and Bebi were able to organise everything before we catch up with them." With the decision now taken, the advanced couple set off without delay and were soon out of sight.

We followed at the best pace we could manage, although it was soon obvious that it would take us twice as long to reach the coast than it will our two colleagues. I held on to Khumit's arm to try and give her some support, but suddenly her legs gave way and she tumbled to the ground. "What's the matter, did you trip over something?" I asked her.

"No, it's just that I've no strength left to walk," she replied, trying to hold back the sobs. "I'm sorry but I can't continue. It's important that you catch up with the others rather than delay whilst waiting for me to rest. Please go now; I'm sure I shall be able to manage on my own."

"Khumit, as I said before, I shall not leave you here alone. After you've taken all the time you need to recover some of your strength we shall together walk the short distance back to Shakir and Bennu's farm. Once we're safely there, that will be the time to decide what to do next."

The sobs could be held back no longer and the tears ran down her cheeks. "Thank you so much my dear Metjen," was all she could manage to say whilst trying to dry her face with her long hair. We sat on the grass for more than an hour, largely in silence.

"Do you think you are now able to start walking to the farm?" I asked her gently.

"I shall try," she replied bravely. Putting my arm around her waste I helped her stand and then supported her as we walked slowly back along the path. After nearly an hour of stumbling and pausing we were glad to reach the farm gates again. I called out to Shakir.

"Oh, I didn't expect to see you back here," he said, running over to where we were standing. "It looks like you may have some difficulty." I quickly explained the situation with Khumit's exhaustion, and that we had agreed that the other two members of our party should go on ahead of us.

By this time Bennu had joined us and was looking at Khumit with some concern. "Come inside with me," she said to her. "I shall make up a bed for you so you can rest and become strong again."

The two women went inside, and Shakir said: "What is your plan now, Metjen? Do you also want to come into the house and rest?"

"It's very tempting to accept your kind invitation, but I'm not sure what to do now. I don't want to leave Khumit here by herself, but Bebi and Intef will be wondering if I'm in trouble if I don't join them."

Shakir rubbed his hands over his short beard and paused before speaking. "May I tell you what I'd do faced with your dilemma?"

"Please do so; I would welcome your comments."

"You've told me a lot about your mission, and your Pharaoh expects you to return to him with some information. Your affection for the lovely Khumit is obvious, but what would Senusret think if you returned and told him you'd followed your heart and not his wishes? Remember that we shabtis were created to serve our masters, even though we also have opportunities to enjoy the pleasures of this paradise."

"That's quite a speech, Shakir, and a most necessary one," I responded. "You're quite correct that I've been distracted, and my priority must be to complete my mission. Let me go inside and explain the situation to Khumit, hard though this will be for both of us."

I followed my wise farming friend into his house. Khumit was already resting on a bed in the corner of the main room, with a mug of water in her hand. "How are you feeling now?" I asked.

"Much better now I can rest in comfort,

thank you," she replied. "But you must go now and continue your journey before it's too late."

"That's just what I wanted to talk to you about," I said, taking her hand. "It's a very difficult decision but you have made it easier for me by saying this. If I hurry now I shall be at the coast before nightfall, and can then meet up with the others." Tears started to appear in her eyes again, and it was all I could do to hold back my own. "But I promise I shall come back for you as soon as I possibly can."

Bennu had been keeping a respectful distance but now came toward us. "Don't worry, Metjen, we shall look after Khumit for as long as is necessary, as if she were one of our own family. We'll be glad of her company, and she will be able to help us with the farm work when she's strong enough."

"You are so kind," I said. If it's all agreed, then I must leave right away." Bennu and Shakir discretely turned away whilst I embraced the girl that I now knew I loved. Without another word I left the farm and hurried back along the path to the coast, with many thoughts competing for attention in my mind.

Although I too was feeling the physical effects of the exertion of the last few days, I managed to keep going with just occasional brief stops and, by late afternoon, reached the jetty with the boats tied up alongside. Where were Bebi and Intef? Had they already left and rowed across to Flower Island? I looked around to see if there was anyone I could ask, and saw a man approaching the boats whilst carrying two large baskets of farm produce.

"Greetings," I said, walking toward him. "I'm looking for two of my friends who should have arrived here earlier today. One is tall and muscular with a beard whilst the other is clean shaven and wears a skullcap. Have you seen anyone like these?"

"Yes, I did see two strangers here who could have been those you described. We had a short conversation but they seemed impatient and kept looking back along the inland path."

"That could be them, I agree, and they were probably trying to see me coming to join them. But they aren't here now. Have you any idea where they could be? Perhaps they could have left this island in one of the boats."

The man shook his head. "That's unlikely. I've made several trips here today, bringing baskets of cheese from my farm so that my partner can take them across to Flower Island. Had anyone been anyone rowing away in one of the other boats we would have seen them."

"Thank you, this is useful to know. I should have been with them already but have been delayed longer than they would have expected. Have you any idea where they might be now?"

"If you can't see them walking along the beach then you might wish to take the path I just came along and follow it inland. There are some houses nearby and your friends might have gone there looking for something to eat."

"That is very helpful," I replied. "I shall do as you've suggested. If you happen to see them again could you be so kind as to tell them that I, Metjen, have now arrived."

The man agreed to keep a lookout for my two friends, and I then set off along the path he had indicated. Although Ra still had some way to travel before he disappeared, if I didn't meet Bebi and Intef very soon it would be too dark to risk rowing across to their island today. After only a few minutes I reached the houses the man had mentioned and walked slowly past each one, peering into the front yard to see if anyone was there.

Should I now knock on each door, I wondered, after reaching the last building without success. I'd just started to walk back when I heard a shout coming from the house next to it. "Hey Metjen, we're here!" It was Bebi emerging from the doorway, followed closely by Intef. The three of us quickly came together in the middle of the path. "We saw you from the window when you walked past a moment ago. But where is Khumit?"

"Sorry it has taken me so long to join you but I had to take her back to the farmhouse," I replied. They listened in silence to my account of what happened after they'd gone on ahead this morning, but were obviously concerned.

"This is very unfortunate," Bebi said. "But you did the right thing in leaving Khumit where she will be safe until we can return. We've not been very considerate about what this stressful trip will have taken out of her. At least you are here now, so we can continue the mission. And I have some important news to give you."

"I need something to cheer me up," I replied. "Do tell me."

"When we arrived at the coast we asked everyone we saw if they had encountered Joseph. Because we've learned what he looks like we were able to give them a description."

Bebi paused. "Please do tell me – had anyone seen him? I asked."

"Ah, you are impatient Metjen, as usual! But yes, he was here yesterday. Shortly after he arrived he took one of the boats and set off in the direction of Flower Island. So you see, we are now only one day behind him."

"Wonderful, at last we're making progress. If we set off right away we shall surely be able to catch up with Joseph and offer him the Pharaoh's protection."

"I agree," Bebi replied. "The farmer who lives in the house we just came from very kindly gave us some food. If you've not eaten since you set off, you must also have something in order to keep your strength up. We would want you to suffer the same fate that Khumit has."

Although I wasn't too happy to be thought of as someone who might collapse from the lack of sustenance, he was right in urging me not to neglect the essential need for food. Intef went back into the house and returned shortly afterwards with some bread, cheese and fruit. "You can eat this when we're in the boat if you wish to save time," he said.

The three of us walked back to the jetty, climbed into one of the boats and cast off. Bebi looked up to the sky. "It'll be nearly dark by the time we reach our destination. Perhaps we should have found a safe place to spend the night on Animal Island and waited until tomorrow morning before making the journey."

"But that would then have put us two days behind Joseph and we could have lost his trail by the time we arrived," I said in between mouthfuls of the food. "As soon as I've finished eating I'll take my turn to row. I'm sure we'll make landfall whilst there's still be enough light to find shelter."

Half an hour passed by with little discussion as we saved our breath for the rowing. But then Bebi spoke up: "We don't seem to making much progress. By this time we should be half way across the channel but are still close to where we started."

Intef stared at the sea and then up at the clouds. "The weather appears to be changing and we are rowing into a wind that is growing stronger. To make maters worse the tide is also against us. We need to decide whether to continue on toward our destination or turn back to Animal Island."

"If we return to where we started we shall have wasted another day," I said. "Perhaps we can press on with renewed effort and hope that conditions will improve as quickly as they deteriorated. But what do you think, Bebi?"

"I know how important this mission is to you, Intef, especially as we now seem to be coming closer to finding Joseph. In other circumstances I would have recommended turning back but, if you and Intef understand the risk of continuing onwards, then I'll go along with you."

Intef nodded his consent, so the three of us took hold of the oars again and rowed on in silence. Another half hour went by and I had to admit that we had progressed no further than the mid-way point between the two islands. The wind had become stronger, it was growing dark, and we were close to exhaustion. We stopped rowing to try and get our breath back.

"I'm sorry, my friends, but it's looking like my keenness to continue may have put us all in difficulty," I said. "We should have done what you thought was best, Bebi, but we're now faced with the same options as before. Should we continue onwards or return to Animal Island?"

"Please don't take this all on yourself, Metjen, as we did all agree on what to do. We didn't know then that the wind and the waves would conspire against us. But, as you said, what do we do now?"

"I can probably continue rowing for a while, but it's doubtful we would reach our destination tonight," Intef said.

"And whichever island we spend the night on, assuming we can make landfall on either, we shall be in danger if the gods decide to wage their battles over where we have camped," Bebi added.

"We'd surely be no safer if we stayed in mid channel," I commented. "Bebi, you are a more experienced traveller than am I so please tell us what you recommend."

"Alright. If we turn around and head for Animal Island, the wind and current will be behind us. At least we can try to reach land there even if it's dark, rather than stay here or continue forward. We'll just have to accept that we've reduced our chance to catch up with Joseph for the moment, but we can continue with the quest tomorrow if the elements permit." No discussion was needed, and we headed back the way we had so laboriously just come.

Although the rowing was easier with the wind at our backs, we again did not seem to be making any progress. "Is it just my imagination, or is something diverting us from our intended direction?" I asked the others. "Although it's now dark, the few lights we can see on the island keep moving away to the left and we have to keep adjusting our course."

"Yes, I was also starting to notice this," Bebi replied. "We need to rest for a few minutes, so let's see what happens when we stop rowing." Glad of the chance to recover from our exertion we pulled in the oars.

Our small boat started to turn to the right until we were facing the opposite direction. Then the lights of Animal Island came back into view. "The current is taking us around in a wide circle!" Intef exclaimed. "Look over the side, and you'll see the water swirling around us."

"We're being caught up in a giant whirlpool and it could become dangerous if the intensity increases," Bebi said. "I've heard about these from the local fishermen. If the current between the two islands is strong and a powerful wind is blowing, a maelstrom forms and small craft like ours can be sucked down to the seabed. There is no escape."

My anguish at having exposed my friends to this latest danger added to the fear of perishing beneath the waves. "You should not have listened to my urgings to press on rather than spend another night on Animal Island. I'm responsible for what could be a tragic end to this mission for all of us."

"We came willingly," Bebi said. "And this is not the time to feel sorry for yourself, Metjen. The question now is what can we do to try and save ourselves?"

"I too have spoken with those who have had the experience of being caught in these whirlpools," said Intef. "They say there are only two actions you can try, neither of which might prevent disaster but could allow time for the wind and tide to die down."

"And what are they?" I shouted in desperation.

"The first is to throw everything out of the boat to lighten it as much as possible. This slows down the rate of descent a little. The second is to row in the opposite direction to the spin of the water, which might enable you to keep near the surface. But neither will save you if the whirlpool is strong and long-lasting."

"Thank you, Intef; this at least gives us something to do, so let's get on with it. What can we discard to lighten the boat?" We looked around but there was little we could throw over the side – a spare oar, one of the wooded bench seats, and the anchor along with its chain. Although very weary, we reversed the direction in which we were sitting and started to row against the swirling current.

By now it was completely dark apart from the twinkling stars up above, but we could just make out the wooden items we'd discarded moving lower and lower down the funnel of the maelstrom. If this was not disconcerting enough, we started to hear a rumbling noise from the heavens and it was coming closer. The gods had begun their nightly battle and it would soon be right over our heads. We were completely exposed with nowhere to hide. I was sure our mission was about to come to a tragic end.

"It doesn't look as if we are significantly slowing our descent into the abyss," Bebi shouted above the noise. Can we row any faster?"

"I'm close to exhaustion and must stop whatever the consequences," I replied. Intef was pulling away valiantly but I could see that he too could not continue for much longer. We tried to keep going but, with our strength gone, one by one we let go of the oars and let the boat drift along on its own. The fighting was now right above our heads and we could see flashes of light in the sky. Our situation appeared hopeless: our mission and probably our very existence were surely coming to an end.

"We have to lighten the boat still further!" Intef shouted. "There's only one option left." Without another word he leapt over the side of the boat and was soon being swept away from us.

"No! No!" Bebi and I called out, leaning over and trying to grab hold of our courageous friend who was martyring himself in the hope that we would survive. But, whilst his selfless action had succeeded in slowing the boat's downward spiral, we now had no hope of reaching him.

Before the two of us could recover from the shock of Intef's sudden departure we became aware of a dark shape bearing down upon us. Just in time we ducked out of the way of a large flying snake that was about to sink its fangs into us. It was the God Apopis. He had broken away from his nightly battle with Ra and was seizing the chance to take advantage of our vulnerability, adrift on the sea below. He turned and was ready to strike again.

This is the end, I thought. Stuck in a

whirlpool, with one of our party now at the mercy of the sea and the other two of us being attacked by an evil god. I deserved to perish but not my friends who would be enjoying their normal lives if I hadn't intervened. Closing my eyes and crouching as low as I could in this little boat, I waited for the inevitable to happen.

I heard the sound of flapping wings, and then a wicked cackling very close to me. Apopis was above my head but then he suddenly cried out in pain. I looked up and saw Ra. He was pointing a finger at his arch enemy and projecting a stream of bright particles into its body. The Snake God rapidly departed, shrieking that he would one day have his revenge.

"I am so grateful you came to save us yet again," I said to Ra. "Without your help both of us would surely now be dead."

"It is indeed fortunate that I looked down and saw that you were in trouble," he replied. "But where are the other members of your party?"

"Khumit is safe with farmers on Animal Island, but Intef jumped over the side moments ago to give Bebi and me a better chance of surviving in this maelstrom."

Ra did not immediately reply but went straight down into the whirlpool, returning a minute later carrying the body of Intef. "Is he still alive?" Bebi asked as the god gently deposited his friend into the boat.

"You will have to see for yourself," Ra said. "But I must be away now before my enemies discover where I am and continue their battle with me. I shall speak with my ally Amon, the God of Air, and ask him to calm the wind so that you will be able to continue your journey safely" We shouted our thanks as our saviour sped back into the night sky, and then turned our attention to Intef.

Again I asked Bebi: "Is Intef still alive?"

"I can't say yet," he replied, bending over the inert body of our friend. "He's not breathing but I'm sure his heart is still beating. Let's take turns to push on his chest to see if we can get him to cough up the water he must have breathed in."

We immediately started the emergency treatment, hoping it was not too late to save this brave shabti. It didn't bring immediate results but, just as we were about to admit defeat, we were overjoyed to hear him splutter and then regurgitate a large amount of water. He eventually opened his eyes and looked around. "Where am I?" he asked. "Am I dead?"

"No, you're back on the boat with Bebi and me," I replied, quickly explaining Ra's intervention that saved us all. "It was very heroic of you to be willing to sacrifice yourself for our sake, but perhaps also a little foolhardy for not discussing it with us first before you jumped into the sea."

"There was no time for any discussion," he said. "I could see that the boat would soon disappear under the waves and it was important that you'd be able to continue with your mission."

I put my hand onto his shoulder. "We are indebted to for this, Intef. It was an unselfish act but we'd have been devastated to lose you. We are overjoyed that you were rescued just in time."

"Are we still descending into the whirlpool?" he asked. "I don't detect any movement of the boat."

"Apart from rescuing you, and saving us from being eaten by the wicked Apopis, Ra said he would ask Amon to calm the wind so that the waves would cease and the whirlpool would lose its power," Bebi answered. "It seems to be working because we're now back on the surface and the storm has just about ceased."

"This is he second time the Sun God has saved us from certain death, but we can't assume he'll always be there in our times of need," I said. "It's important that we always take steps to protect ourselves from possible danger. Now that we're safe, we need to decide what to do next."

"I suggest we just stay here until dawn,"

Bebi answered. "The fighting gods have moved away and the sea is calm. We're now safe. Intef needs time to recover, and we could all benefit from some rest. In the morning we'll be able to continue our journey to Flower Island and see if we can obtain any news about Joseph."

No one dissented, so we made ourselves as comfortable as possible within the confines of our small craft and allowed ourselves the luxury of some relaxation.

Chapter 7

Parting and Meeting

We were roused from our dozing by the first rays of the sun glinting above the horizon. "Are you strong enough to start rowing again?" I asked Intef. "If you'd like more time to recover, Bebi and I will be able to manage on our own."

"Thank you, but I feel fine now," he replied. "Let's be on our way; we shall soon reach our island and be able to gather some food to eat." We took up our positions and rowed at a steady pace in the now mercifully calm sea. In less than an hour we landed on Flower Island, the home of my two companions. The pleasure of arriving safely competed with the sadness I felt that the fourth member of our party was not with us. I wondered if I would I ever see the lovely Khumit again.

Before continuing inland Intef went to gather some honeycomb from the same bees nest as he did on our outward journey, whilst Bebi and I collected some dates and palm nuts. These items sufficed to renew our energy and we then started walking toward where my companions knew there were houses. "Hello there!" Bebi cheerfully called out as we arrived at the first one. He and Intef exchanged greetings with the two shabtis who came out to meet us, and I was then introduced to them.

"We're wondering if you have seen a man we are seeking," I said. "He is a resurrected one, and his name is Joseph; he's a tall and imposing figure with grey hair and beard."

"Indeed we have seen someone like this," one of them answered. "He passed by here just two days ago and we spoke with him."

"That's good to hear. Was he asking questions?"

"His main need was for some food, which we gladly gave him. The poor man said he'd not had anything to eat for two days, as he was forced to keep moving."

"It is indeed the man we're looking for," I commented. "We know he's trying to avoid capture by three wicked men, and we wish to offer him protection."

"Yes, those three were also here, a day before Joseph. They were asking everyone if they'd seen him but nobody had at that time, and we probably wouldn't have admitted it if we had.

They have since returned to Animal Island and must have passed close to Joseph somewhere on their travels, so it's fortunate he was not seen and captured."

"Do you know where he is now?" Bebi asked.

"No, he just said he'd have to keep moving. If you keep going in the same direction as he was walking, you might be able to discover where he could be."

We thanked the shabtis and continued on our journey. Just like the time I was last here, I was again captivated by both the beautiful colours and the fragrances of the flowers that gave this island its name. "As we've arrived here quite early in the morning, we'll be able to reach our own home by nightfall if we don't linger too long in any one place," said Bebi. This was welcome news, as it would be so nice to be able to relax safe and sound in familiar surroundings again after our traumatic experience last night.

Every time we came to a farmhouse we stopped and asked the same question of the people we saw, and received similar answers to those of the first one. Yes, Joseph had been there; no, they did not know where he was now. When we were half way back to the palace I said: "There's another house just ahead of us. After we've questioned the residents there we need to decide what to do next, as it looks like the trail we're following has now gone cold."

"I agree with you," Bebi responded. "It's just a pity we lost a day stranded by that whirlpool, otherwise now we'd only be just behind Joseph."

We arrived at the farm gate and asked the shabti there the same question about Joseph's whereabouts, expecting the same answer. "Indeed, he was here only two days ago," he answered.

"Did he say where he'd go next?" Bebi asked.

"The poor man was unable to continue. He is old and not strong any more, and what he told me he had endured over the last few weeks filled me with pity. I immediately invited him into the house and my wife and I gave him food. He then lay down to sleep and only awoke when morning came."

This was indeed encouraging information. "That was very kind of you," I said. "Joseph is a good man, and we are here to try and help rid him of his adversaries for ever. What was his condition yesterday morning?"

"He said he was much refreshed and ready to continue his journey. We gave him food again, and he then left us."

"Did he say where he was going?"

"No, only that he needed to keep moving to

avoid the fate he knew the evil trio had in store for him. The poor man deserves a permanent home where he can live in peace."

"This is just what my Pharaoh can give him," I said. "You've been very helpful, thank you. We must now try and catch up with Joseph before those vindictive three men do. We're now only one day behind him."

Bebi, Intef and I resumed our journey, buoyed on by this latest news. "I wonder where he could be now," Bebi said. "According to what the farmer has told us, we should be able to travel faster than Joseph can, so every step will take us closer to him."

"This is your home island and you'll know where all the paths are. How many different routes could he have taken from the farmhouse?" I asked.

"There are tracks around the coast and straight across the middle of the island," Bebi replied. "Although we don't know which one Joseph might have taken, we've no choice today but to take the shortest way back to our home in the palace grounds before the gods start their nightly jousting. If we don't have any confirmation from those we meet along the way that he went in that direction, we can explore some of the other routes tomorrow."

We walked in the direction Bebi indicated

but I was concerned that, if Joseph had not taken this path, we might lose his trail yet again after only being one day behind him. There were only a few houses along this pathway, but we called at each one and asked all whom we saw if they had encountered Joseph. Nobody said they had seen him, so it was becoming more likely that he must have gone in another direction after he landed here.

The afternoon was drawing to a close as we approached Queen Nefret's palace and then walked across the grounds to the large house shared by Bebi and his friends. The front door opened before we reached it and the three shabtis who had remained there rushed out to greet us.

"Thank you for your welcome my friends, it's good to back here with you. We have a lot to report," said Bebi, clasping each of them in turn.

We went inside but, before we could sit down to rest, one of the residents asked: "Where is Khumit – is she following on behind you?"

I felt it only right that I answered. "I'm sorry to have to tell you that I had to leave her on Animal Island. She was too exhausted to walk any further." I could see the horrified look all three had on their faces, so quickly continued. "Please don't be alarmed, she's in the good care of a kindly farmer and his wife, and will be able to help them in their work once she's recovered her strength. I am sure that eventually she'll return to you."

"Of course I'll have to explain her absence to Queen Nefret, and hope she won't be angry at what we anticipate will only be a temporary absence of one of her trusted servants," Bebi added.

Whilst it was clear that this had not pleased our three friends, they allowed the matter to end there, at least for the present. There was a lot of news to exchange, and Bebi summarised where we had been and what we'd discovered, including the great courage Intef had shown in his willingness to sacrifice himself to save him and me from perishing in the whirlpool.

"Although we know Joseph had visited our island, and might still be here, unfortunately he still evades us," he concluded. "None of the neighbours we passed on our journey here today said they'd seen him. Tomorrow we'll have to explore the other paths. As we know this homeland of ours well, perhaps we can split up and each take a different route. We can then meet back at the house to share what we've discovered."

Intef had so far been content to leave the reporting to Bebi and me, but now commented: "I agree, it's a good idea, Bebi. But we have been very active for more than a week now, sometimes with little sleep or food. What we need now is a good meal and a peaceful night behind closed doors. In the morning we can finalise our plans."

This was quite a speech from the strong man of our group who had endured all that befell us without complaining. But of course he was correct, and any further discussion about our past adventures and future plans was suspended. We gladly accepted the offer of our three friends for us to sit down and relax whilst they prepared one of the best evening meals we could have hoped for.

After we'd finished, we found it difficult to keep our eyes open so we stumbled into the bed chamber and flopped down to enjoy a night's sleep. If the gods had been engaged in their battles above our heads, we would not have been aware of it.

We awoke much refreshed as Ra commenced his daily passage across the heavens, and discussed our plans whilst eating the first meal of the day. "Last night we agreed to split up and explore other paths, "Bebi said. "There's only one route down to the coast on the other side of the island, and it then divides to left and right. If you, Metjen, and Intef reconnoitre these two, I will visit the houses in the area around the palace. We can meet up back here at mid-day to give our reports and then decide what to do next."

No further discussion was needed, and the three of us set off as soon as we'd finished our meal. "Are you sure you've now fully recovered from your ordeal in the whirlpool two nights ago?" I asked Intef as we walked along at a brisk pace.

"Please don't worry about me," he replied. "I'm strong and able to face whatever is required of me." I just hoped he was being realistic, but we soon reached the coast and the two of us then continued on in different directions.

There were very few people about but those I spoke with said they had not seen the man we were seeking. I was wondering whether or not I should turn around to wait for Intef at the crossroads, when I saw a fisherman beaching his small boat after trying his luck on the open water. "Greetings," I said. "Have you caught anything today?"

"Just one fish that my wife and I can eat tonight," he replied. I then posed the question I'd asked of many others, up to now only receiving negative responses. "I might have seen this man," he said. "When I was tying up my boat yesterday morning a stranger came out of the bushes. He was a tall, distinguished man with a grey beard. When I spoke with him he said he'd spent the night there in the open wrapped in his cloak."

"That certainly sounds like Joseph," I said,

perhaps with too much excitement in my voice.

"Did he say where he was going?"

"I first gave him some bread I had left over from what my wife had given me when I went out early to fish. Although he was doing his best to maintain a dignified composure, the poor man was obviously starving."

"That was kind of you, but did he say where he was going to next?"

"I was coming to that," the fisherman replied with a slight smile at my impatience. "We chatted together for a while and he said he had to keep moving, going from one island to another. He was planning to walk to the jetty and take a boat across to Arable Island."

"Thank you, that's very helpful news, and I'll go back now and share this with my colleagues," I said. "Our mission is to give him sanctuary and defeat his enemies. Farewell."

I hurried off to where Intef and I had gone our separate ways. It's still earlier than the time we agreed to return to the house and he probably won't be there yet, so I proceeded along the path he had taken in the hope of meeting him. But it was another half an hour before I saw him walking in my direction.

"What are you doing here?" he asked. "I thought we were going in opposite directions."

"I did, but now have some promising news

to report," I said.

"And I have some that is not good. Which shall we share first – the good or the bad?"

This unexpected statement quickly deflated my excitement. "Oh dear, but I'll tell you what I learned a short time ago. A fisherman told me that Joseph had spent the night under the trees near the beach two nights ago, and he was intending to row across to my island that very morning. Thus we are once again only one day behind him."

"Yes, that's interesting to hear," Intef commented with a joyless voice. "But what I've just been told is that Hepzefa, Neferu and Simontu had been seen this morning landing on the other side of this island. It seems they'd heard Joseph was also here and immediately set off to catch him. It's fortunate you know he has just left here, but it will surely not take this wicked trio long to also find this out, and they'll doubtless immediately follow."

"I agree, this is worrying, and the gap is closing for both us and them. But at least we know where both of the parties are now. We must return to your house as quickly as we can now to discuss what to do with this latest information."

We retraced our steps, arriving at the palace grounds by midday and sought out Bebi. "I've visited several houses in the vicinity but not learned anything new," he said. "You two are back earlier than I'd expected so you must have something to report."

"Indeed we have," I replied. "Firstly, I heard that Joseph spent last night near the beach here but he's probably now left to go over to Arable Island. Secondly, Intef discovered that the three vindictive men landed on the other side of your island this morning. We must now quickly decide what to do, which is why the two of us have returned."

Bebi paused whist he absorbed this summary of what we'd learned this morning. "It's important that Joseph is found and receives the protection he needs before the three men get to him. This means going over to your island, Metjen."

"I agree, and we must leave right away if we're to reach the coast and row across before nightfall. We don't want to suffer the same trauma as we had reaching here."

"Yes, that's the right thing to do," Bebi said. "But you will have to go alone. Remember that we are in the service of Queen Nefret and could only be away from the palace for two weeks. Although there's still a little time remaining, if we come with you and have to spend days chasing after Joseph and are late returning, we'll be in serious trouble. As it is I still have to try to explain to the Queen why Khumit has not returned. I am sorry, Metjen."

I had selfishly forgotten that these shabtis who had helped me so much only had a limited time, and just assumed we would remain a team. "It is I who am sorry, Bebi, for taking things for granted," I replied. "I shall always be grateful, and will do my best to meet you all again when this mission is over. But, reluctantly, I have to go now if I'm to reach my home island whilst Ra is still in the heavens."

"It's been an exciting time for each of us, and we all want Joseph to evade capture and the three men stopped," said Bebi. "If we have the opportunity we shall delay them to give you a better chance of finding Joseph before they do. But just wait for two minutes whilst I quickly pack some food for you to take with you on your journey home."

Whilst I waited, Intef took off his belt with the knife in its sheath and gave it to me. "Here, take this Metjen. You may need it and I shall be able to obtain another one from the palace workshop."

"Thank you so much, my friend. This is yet another kind gesture you've all bestowed on me during the last week," I said as I tied the belt around my waist. Bebi then came back with a parcel of food and, after a warm embrace with each of these kind and helpful shabtis, I left them and hurried off down to the coast for the second time today.

Arriving at the jetty, feeling rather breathless after walking faster than was comfortable for me, I was pleased to see several craft of different sizes tied up there. As I was on my own, I selected the smallest one and set of for my home island. No time to eat the food I'd been given now, I thought, as I need to make the crossing before it's dark. But I was not prepared for the effort required to row the boat on my own whilst trying to remain on course. My fatigue increased with every stroke and I had no alternative but to stop for a brief rest.

I ate a little of the food but realised that the tide appeared to be pushing the boat back to where it started from. Wearily, I resumed rowing as best as I could but wasn't confident I had sufficient strength remaining to complete my journey. Was this going to be another night at the mercy of the sea, as it was when we were caught in the whirlpool? That mustn't happen, especially as I was now on my own. I tried to ignore the pain invading my body and concentrated with a single mind on pulling the oars.

At last, with the light was almost gone, I felt the keel of the boat scrape against the sand. Taking hold of the mooring rope I staggered onto the beach and collapsed into unconsciousness. I didn't know for how long I'd remained in this state, but gradually became aware of a noise. It came from above and sounded as if people were shouting and yelling at each other. It was coming closer. Suddenly I was fully awake. Oh no! It was the gods enjoying their nightly battle, and I was exposed and alone.

The rope was still in my hand, and I managed to drag the boat another yard up the beach so that it wouldn't float away, and then staggered into the shrubbery to hide. Had I been seen? The commotion was now right above my head. I kept very still, hardly daring even to breath. Thankfully, a few minutes later the noise gradually moved away. Realising that I could so easily have been caught had I delayed even a few seconds more, I decided to remain hidden where I was until morning. Fatigue soon took over again, and I lapsed into sleep.

I was awakened by the bright light of Ra shining on my face as he began his daily passage across the sky. Stiff from lying on the uneven ground, my clothing damp from the wet grass, I stood up and stretched. Grateful that I was now safe and on my home island, I was keen to begin my search for Joseph. Once the three men discovered that he was no longer on Flower Island they would certainly come over here. I hoped that Bebi and Intef would be able to delay them to give me some more time to find him first.

Returning to where I'd beached the boat I managed to pull it forward a little further and tied the rope to a thick tree branch that I pushed into the sand as far as I could. I hadn't managed to reach the mooring jetty the previous night, and it was one of the rules of using these vessels that we must always leave them secured. After reaching inside to retrieve the parcel of food I started walking. I knew most of the paths on this island, so headed for the one that would take me back to my home.

As before, my intention was to ask all those I encountered along the way if they had seen Joseph. Eventually I came to the path and started to follow it inland. Then I saw a man scooping water to drink from a small stream that was nearing the end of its journey to the sea. "Greetings, my friend," I called out to him. "Can I please speak with you for a moment?"

He turned and started to walk toward me. I could immediately see he was not a fellow shabti but a resurrected one. He was tall and grey haired, and the blue cloak around him was creased and mud stained. "Certainly," he replied gently. "What do you wish to tell me?"

I opened my mouth but no sound came out. Could this possibly be the man I've been seeking? No, surely not, it would be too much of a coincidence. "I'm looking for someone who came to this island two days ago, and am asking everyone I meet if they've seen him."

"Tell me, why is it important that you discover the whereabouts of this person?" he asked.

This was no time for any more carefully guarded responses, I decided. There is no alternative but to state my purpose and hope that it will be favourably received. "My name is Metjen, and I have been sent out by my master, Pharaoh Senusret the third, to seek out any troubles that will disrupt the peace of this paradise."

"I see," he replied. "And if you do find something to report to him, what action will he take?"

"He will wish to use force to quell it."

"Will this not be just to satisfy his desire to be a warrior, and then be able to justify it to Osiris as being a noble action intended to avoid a wider conflict?"

It was clear this man was well informed, and wanted to hear the truth from me without any attempt to disguise it. "You are correct, Sir, but it would surely serve both purposes."

He nodded. "You told me you were seeking someone who came to this island. If you find this person, what will you then do?"

"I know he's in trouble and is trying to avoid being captured. I would offer him the protection of the Pharaoh."

"I see. And what is the name of this man?"

"His name is Joseph, and he is fleeing from Hepzefa, Neferu and Simontu," I said, relieved that at last the games were over and plain speaking could begin.

"I am that person you are seeking to help," Joseph replied. "It is true that I have had to keep running but I am now growing weary of this. I have to trust what you have just told me, even if it turns out to be a trap to hold me here until the three who wish to do me harm find me."

"It's no trap," I assured him. "I'm overjoyed to have found you whilst there is still time, as I have heard that those who wish to take their revenge on you are now on Flower Island. When they know you're no longer there they'll certainly come here. Let me take you to my master without delay."

"Thank you Metjen, I shall accompany you. But first I just need to rest for a short time. I had to sleep outdoors by the stream last night, and I cannot remember the last time I had something to eat apart from what I could pick from the trees during my travels."

"Of course we can stop for a while, and we

can share the food I have with me," I said, relieved to have at last encountered Joseph and that he'd agreed to come with me. "There's much I wish to tell you about the events of the past week, and about the adventures my friends from Flower Island and I have experienced whilst trying to find you."

"And there is also a lot I can relate to you about what I have experienced," Joseph said as he hungrily devoured the bread and cheese I passed to him.

"We should arrive at my house soon after midday," I commented when we had resumed our journey. "I have three companions there and you'll be safe inside with them whilst I go and report to the Pharaoh."

"That will be so welcome after having to constantly be on the move," he replied. "I am so grateful that you and your friends have endured so much in order to help me. But it is sad that you have had to leave them behind, and especially Khumit you told me about who is not even in her own home. Perhaps one day I will be able to repay you for all your kindness."

As we walked along, chatting like two old friends and responding to each others questions, my mind went back to when I commenced my mission less than two weeks ago. Again the beauty of this place enveloped me, with the bird song, colourful blossoms, and the corn growing in the fields swaying to the music of the gentle breeze. We passed the same river as I did on my outward journey, where the local fishermen were trying their luck for pleasure rather than food.

Our pace slowed due to the weariness we both felt as a consequence of our recent deprivations but, by mid afternoon, my dwelling at last came into sight. "We are here," I said joyfully to my companion as we entered through the front door. I introduced Joseph to the three other residents, and briefly explained why he was here. "Let's sit and rest, and have something to eat before we do anything else" I suggested. My friends hurried off to the kitchen to prepare some food for us.

It was good to have a substantial meal and then relax with a mug of beer whilst Joseph and I reported to my fellow residents and answered their many questions. But by the time we'd finished the daylight had almost gone. "It's too late for me to go now to my master," I said. "He is never in a good mood at this time of day and it will be better to wait until morning."

Addressing Joseph I added: "My companions and I will make up a bed for you, and you can remain with us for as long as you wish."

"Thank you all for your hospitality," he

replied. "It will be wonderful to be safe and comfortable after such a long time running away from those who wish to do me harm."

It was indeed a relief to have a peaceful, undisturbed sleep again without having to worry about the warring gods. We awoke refreshed the following morning and Joseph and I replaced our stained garments with clean ones. After we'd eaten, I made my way across to the palace and asked the guard to tell my master that his Vizier had returned and had some news for him. A short while later I was ushered into the audience chamber.

Chapter 8

Jeopardy

"I had expected you back before this, Metjen, where have you been all this time?" the Pharaoh asked without any pleasantries or welcome.

"Sir, I have already visited three of the other islands to see if there were any threats to the peace of this land, just as you instructed me to do. I met with some of the residents from Flower Island and they accompanied me for much of my travels. We experienced danger on more than one occasion, and it was only the intervention of Lord Ra that saved us. My companions told me that Joseph, who had been appointed Viceroy by your father Senusret the Second, was in danger."

"Yes, I was only a young boy at the time, but I do recall him. Why is he in danger now?"

I was pleased my master had remembered Joseph, and that he seemed to be interested in what I had to say. "If you remember this man, were you aware there were those who were jealous he had been appointed over their heads to a senior position at the court?"

The Pharaoh remained silent whilst he presumably cast his mind back to those early days. "Indeed, I do remember there were those who resented him, especially because he wasn't an Egyptian by birth. But you still need to tell me why he's in trouble now."

"Of course Sir, I'm coming to that. Three of those who harboured a grudge against him then were resurrected and they now live on Lake Island. Their names are Hepzefa, Nefferu and Simontu. They could not take their revenge on Joseph when they were at court because he was under the protection of your father. But here in this afterlife he's alone and vulnerable. They are seeking him now so they can carry out their evil wishes. He has to be constantly on the move, but one day he'll surely be caught by this vindictive trio and that will be the end of him."

I wondered if my master would indicate whether or not he was sympathetic toward Joseph and his plight. If he was not, then my mission would have failed and my house guest would be unable to remain. "That would be unfortunate," Senusret replied. "My father always spoke highly of him. Do you know where he is now?"

Much relieved I answered, "For most of my journey from one island to the next he was always at least one day ahead of me. I then heard he was heading here. My companions had to remain on Flower Island to continue serving their Queen, so I came back on my own. After spending a night in the open air I came across a man who had done the same, and was overjoyed to discover that it was Joseph."

"That was indeed fortunate," the Pharaoh replied, now apparently interested in what I had to say. "I would like to meet this Joseph; can you bring him to me?"

"Sir, I took the liberty of taking him to my house last evening and we shared our food with him. He then spent a restful night safely indoors for the first time in many weeks. I can go and bring him to you right away if you wish. But I should first tell you that the three men who are seeking Joseph may already be making their way toward our island. They will then search for him and carry out their threat."

"It's good you have told me all this, Metjen; it seems that this unfortunate man is being unfairly persecuted and deserves some protection. Go now and return with him in one hour. We can then all discuss this matter together."

I left the palace and walked back to my house feeling a sense of relief. This was now working out even better than I'd hoped. Senusret did seem genuinely interested in the welfare of

Joseph, so perhaps he had good memories of him when he was in the service of his father. But then he could just be thinking this was a good opportunity to fulfil his desire to be a warrior leader, as he was during his earthly existence.

Joseph was anxiously waiting to hear my report as soon as I entered the door. "Is the Pharaoh angry with you for sheltering me in your home without first seeking his permission? Is he going to hand me over to those who wish to do me harm?"

"Do not be concerned, my friend," I assured him. "My master appears to be sympathetic to your plight even if it may be partly motivated by his wish to engage in some forceful peacekeeping. He was only a child when you were Viceroy but he does remember you and that there were those who resented your appointment."

"This is certainly is a great relief," he said, clearly reflecting this in his countenance. "What is his plan now – did he give you any instructions concerning me?"

"Not yet. But he wishes to talk with us both in just less than one hour from now, so I suggest we make ourselves as presentable as we can and be prepared to answer his questions."

We made sure we were clean and tidy, and discussed what might be said to us whilst we waited for the appointed time to proceed to the palace. "Right Joseph, it's time to go and see what Senusret has to say to us." As soon as we arrived we were ushered through to the Pharaoh's private chamber."

"Welcome to Arable Island," my master said in a friendly tone that was rare to hear coming from his lips. "I was only a young boy when you entered my father's court but I do remember you as a kindly man who was a great help to him."

"Thank you, Pharaoh Senusret, I am honoured to hear you say this," Joseph replied. "I also remember you. I recall that you were rather headstrong and often in trouble fighting with the other boys."

It was interesting for me to hear this, and it seems that my master had changed little since those days. He's still spoiling for a fight but now he has to be careful and not upset Osiris or the judges who allowed him to enter this paradise.

The Pharaoh continued: "Metjen has given me a brief account of his meeting with you yesterday, and your plight. I would like to hear in more detail from you why you find yourself in this predicament."

"Certainly, sir, I shall be pleased to do so. Because you were only young at the time I served your father, you may not have been aware that there were those who were jealous of my appointment. They were already jostling for promotion and were most unhappy when I was given the senior role, especially as I was an outsider."

"Yes, I do have some memory of this, but I can recall my father telling me he was very impressed with your ability to interpret dreams. Because you'd correctly predicted the famine, he was able to take the necessary action to save stocks of grain during the time of plenty to sustain the population during the time of need. Without this action we would all have starved to death."

"It was only a gift that I cannot explain," Joseph replied modestly. "But I was pleased to be of service to the Pharaoh instead of languishing in prison. After I left my earthly life and was admitted to this Field of Reeds, at first I lived comfortably on one of the islands distant from here. Although I did have my enemies in my earthy existence as Viceroy, here in paradise I thought I would be safe."

"But this was not the case, despite the scrutiny of all the resurrected ones by Osiris and the judges," Senusret commented.

"It was for a time, but one by one my enemies must have convinced Osiris they were righteous enough to enter this afterlife. Three of them eventually met and decided to track me down. When they had found me, they would enact the revenge that was inaccessible to them at your father's court."

"So how have you managed to evade these men up to now?"

"I am fortunate there are enough people in this land who remember me from my earthly life, and who have often given me warnings of where these three men are. But I have to be constantly on the move to stay ahead of them. I am no longer young and it is becoming more difficult for me to stay safe. The time is coming closer to when I will be caught, perhaps even betrayed by one of the residents who would have been bribed by my antagonists."

"We must not let this happen to you, Joseph," Senusret replied. "I am glad that Metjen gave you sanctuary, and I will allow this to continue. But Hepzefa and his associates will eventually discover where you are. You would only have to step outside for a moment and they would take you before anyone could stop them. We need to formulate a plan to make sure this will never happen. Go back with Metjen to his house now and stay out of sight. I'll send for you both again when I've decided what action to take."

As we walked away from the palace I couldn't help but be amazed how much Senusret had changed. With me and others he was usually brusque, but with Joseph he was gentle, understanding and helpful.

I mentioned this to my guest, and we could only conclude that it was because my master was only a young boy when Joseph came to the palace. In his position as Viceroy he would have been seen as a senior figure, and both he and the Pharaoh had to be listened to and obeyed. Although my master was now the powerful one, the respect he had for Joseph remained so he continues to treat him with deference. But, whatever the reason, this was a good sign and we must wait to see what he had in store for us.

It was gratifying to see Joseph able to relax and gain strength, now that he had a safe place to stay. Whilst we waited to hear what Senusret would say to us later, he told me more about what his life had been like since he was admitted to this paradise. "Osiris took me to one of the remote islands and said it would be best for me to be away from those who might remember me from my earthly life. I had no complaints as everything I needed was there. The shabtis created for me were there to serve, the accommodation was comfortable and food was plentiful. There were no material things that I lacked."

"So what happened to change this?" I asked.

"Hepzefa, Neferu and Simontu left their earthly life several years after I did. One by one they were resurrected, admitted to the Field of Reeds, and located on Lake Island as the Senior Citizens. They eventually met each other and realised they still had a grievance to settle regarding me. If they hadn't been able to do this whilst on earth, they could try to do so now in this afterlife."

"This was quite a risky objective in view of the fact they had to be judged worthy by Osiris to enter here," I said. "They would certainly be banished or destroyed if they were found to disturb the peace for which this land was created."

Joseph nodded in agreement. "Yes, but they thought they were too clever to be found out. They travelled from island to island, questioning the residents as they went to see if anyone knew where I was living. Eventually I heard they were about to cross over to my home island, and decided that I must leave to avoid being caught. I have been constantly travelling since then and have so far managed to avoid them."

"That is no way to enjoy life in what should be a paradise where we can live in peace," I said. "Wherever my friends from Flower Island and I visited, the residents told us about the three men who had been asking about you. Nobody we saw admitted they had done so, even though some had indeed spoken with you and even given you accommodation."

"I am very grateful to them for not giving me away, and especially to those who provided food shelter. It is obviously why I am still free. But the men are now catching up with me and I am weary of constantly running. I fear that my last chance to avoid capture is here on your island."

"Perhaps it was fate that brought you here and that I was able to find you in time," I responded. "But then the first time we met with Ra he said he would keep watch for anything that might help me with my quest, and maybe he was responsible for our meeting. You'll be safe with us if Senusret can devise a suitable plan to thwart your enemies, so we must now wait until we hear what he has to say."

Senusret did not send for us again on that day, so we continued to take the opportunity to regain our strength and enjoy substantial food. In the evening we updated my three house companions on what had transpired, and then enjoyed a peaceful night's sleep.

* * *

Next morning, whilst we were breaking our fast, the pleasure of meeting up with Joseph and being safely back home started to be replaced by a more realistic evaluation of our situation. In our separate journeys during the previous week both he and my party had managed to remain at least one day ahead of the three evil men. But now, together, we had been at my house for two nights and the last we had heard was that they had landed on Flower Island on the day I had departed from it. If they'd completed their search there, their next action would be to row across here to Arable Island. My master has yet to tell us of his plans, so we could now be in a vulnerable situation.

I shared my thoughts with Joseph. "Yes, you are correct, and we need to remain vigilant if we are not to fail just as a possible resolution of my predicament is in sight," he commented. Further discussion on this was curtailed when a messenger from the palace came to the door to tell us that Senusret had summand us to a meeting with him.

"Today I shall assemble a small band of men armed with spears and knives, and lead them down to the jetty" the Pharaoh began. "We shall see if there is any evidence that Hepzefa and his accomplices have landed on this island. Then we shall visit all the houses in the vicinity and ask if anyone has seen them. If they have arrived here we shall seek them out and order them to leave immediately, never to return. If they disobey we shall attack them with our weapons."

"I'm pleased to hear that you are taking this action to protect Joseph," I replied. "If you don't find evidence that they are already here, what will you do then?"

"Do you think I have not already considered that, Metjen" he said, reverting to the more disagreeable persona I usually experienced when conversing with him. "I shall leave two of my men near the landing place. If they see the boat carrying those three men arriving they are to report to me as fast as they can."

Joseph now responded. "Thank you for taking this action on my behalf. But I would not want you to incur the wroth of Osiris by taking military action in this afterlife that is intended to be peaceful."

"Do not trouble yourself over this," Senusret replied, now back to the benevolent tone he is adopting when conversing with Joseph. "I'm sure I can justify this as a measure to prevent the bloodshed of one who is innocent of any wrongdoing. But there is one more step to add. If I hear that this trio is already here, I shall post a guard outside your house to prevent them entering. We can then take the action against them I mentioned earlier."

There was nothing more to say, so we left

the Pharaoh to carry out his plan and walked back to my house. When we arrived my colleagues had already left to commence their daily work, so we were alone in the building. Looking out into the courtyard we saw my master and twelve of his men march out of the palace and down toward the path that led to the coast. With everyone now away busy with their daily tasks it was strangely quiet outside. It was as if we were the only living creatures in an otherwise deserted village.

With having nothing to occupy ourselves and the need to stay out of sight until this affair was over, time seemed to pass slowly. We made our meals, rested and chatted, looking forward to when my three colleagues returned and could report any developments they might have come across. At long last they joined us again and we locked the door behind them. "Have you any news about the whereabouts of the three men who are seeking Joseph?" I eagerly asked.

One of them, whose name was Theshen, answered on behalf of the others. "No, we were working in the fields for most of the day, and heard nothing."

After the final meal of the day everyone retired for the night. The gods came close with their battle but we remained safely indoors. The next morning, as my house mates were leaving for their work Theshen said, "Be sure to lock the door behind us and don't open it again for anyone but us." We slid the heavy bolt across the door and settled down to what we were sure would be another boring day with nothing to do. But I should have been grateful for the sanctuary after the dangers we'd recently endured. Hopefully, this whole situation will be resolved before too long, I thought.

At midday we were roused from our dozing by someone vigorously knocking on the door. Could this be a trap? I wondered. I went over to it and called out "Who's there?"

"This is Theshen; please open the door. I have some news for you."

I unbolted the door, hoping it would be good news and that we would be free to travel safely again. Theshen entered but then held it open. I was just going to push it shut when he turned around and shouted, "Come in quickly, gentlemen." Three men carrying spears immediately came through the door, and he quickly closed and bolted it again. "I hope nobody saw you arrive," he said to the men who looked strangely familiar.

What on earth is going on? I thought. But, before I could ask, Theshen spoke. "Metjen and Joseph, may I introduce Hepzefa, Neferu and Simontu." I was horrified. The man I thought was a trusted friend had just betrayed us.

"How can you bring yourself to do this?" I asked.

"Sit down and I'll explain before we all leave," he answered with no hint of shame. "But do not try to escape unless you want a spear through your bodies here and now. I heard from a farmer that these people had landed on this island but not at the jetty. They were too clever for that, and were only seen by chance when the farmer noticed them from a distance. He then rushed back to tell somebody."

"And that somebody was you," I said, trying to come to terms with what would probably be a bloody end to my mission.

"You are correct Metjen. I was the first person he saw, and I was separated from my two friends at the time. I asked him not to tell anyone else but to leave it to me to inform those who needed to know, adding that the three men needed to think they had not been observed. They would then be taken by surprise when the Pharaoh is able to find them and take them prisoner."

"But you didn't report this to us or Senusret," I said.

Theshen smiled. He was clearly enjoying his new role as the one in charge. "No I did not. Instead I left my place of work and, following the directions the farmer gave me, set off to find them."

"And obviously you did," Joseph commented whilst remaining commendably calm.

"At first they tried to evade me but I persevered and we eventually came together. I told them I knew who they were but not to be concerned as I was not about to report them to the Pharaoh."

They others had not spoken up to now but, with an evil smile on his face, Hepzefa said: "It's fortunate he did say this because we wouldn't have allowed him to then go away and betray us. Indeed he wouldn't have gone anywhere again!"

Theshen looked a little uncomfortable on hearing this, but continued with his narrative. "I resented having Joseph in our house and told Hepzefa and his friends that I'd be happy if they took him away from us. But then, if I led them to where he was staying, what reward would I receive?"

"This is disgraceful, you are a traitor!" I said moving toward him with my hands raised ready to grab him by the neck. A spear was immediately pushed against my chest and would have penetrated had I continued forward. "Joseph is a virtuous man and has done no harm. Even the Pharaoh acknowledges this. How could you sink so low!"

"I already told you I resented his presence in

this house, and I'm also weary of remaining a servant destined only to carry out orders from others. If there's a chance of being elevated above this, I will do what is necessary to take it."

"And you obviously did," I replied reluctantly, taking a step backwards but still shaking with anger. "What wonderful reward did these three evil creatures offer to turn you into such a disloyal mercenary?"

"They said I'd be appointed to the same position on their island as Joseph was in his earthly life, that of Viceroy. I'd have authority, be able to give orders and use force to ensure they were carried out. Instead of being a servant, I would be a master!"

"You poor, naïve person," I said. "You believed these lies and then brought the men to our house. I hope you obtain a reward, but one that is appropriate to your behaviour and not what you think you've been promised."

"This verbal jousting has gone on long enough," Hepzefa interjected. "We must be on our way back to the coast without being seen. You are coming with us, Metjen; if you try to escape or shout to anyone, it will be the last act you will ever perform."

I had no alternative but to accede to their command. Theshen first went to collect some food in a bag and then opened the door a little and looked outside to see if there was anyone nearby. Satisfied that the area was deserted, the six of us emerged from the house with Joseph and I being sandwiched between two spear-carrying men in front and behind us.

Hepzefa led us into the shelter of the nearest trees as quickly as possible to avoid being seen. Because Theshen knew every inch of this island and was able to give directions to avoid the main paths and any buildings. Apart from these few words of guidance, we marched on in silence. I was still trying to come to terms with this unexpected turn of events, and many competing thoughts were surging through my mind.

Everything was going so well, with Joseph now being safe and the Pharaoh prepared to take action to ensure he would remain so. The last thing I expected was that one of my own house mates would have turned traitor. He was surely gullible in thinking he'd be given the reward he was promised. Once the three men had disposed of Joseph, he would likely suffer he same fate.

But what should I do? When my other two colleagues returned home from work they'd realise something was wrong when Joseph and I were not there. Senusret would quickly be told, and would probably send out a party to find us. I also knew all the little-used tracks on Arable Island and it might be possible to make my escape if the opportunity presented itself. But then would it be right to leave poor Joseph on his own with these evil ones?

Because our progress away from the usual routes was slow, the afternoon was nearly at an end by the time we eventually reached the coast where the three evil ones had left their boat. "Where are you taking us?" I asked Hepzefa as we sat down on the beach to regain our strength.

"To our own place on Lake Island," he replied. "We shall then make Joseph pay for the neglect we endured over all those years in our earthly life when he was Viceroy."

"And am I to suffer the same fate?" I said.

"We'll have to decide what to do with you. It's unfortunate we had to bring you with us, as it was not in our plan. Perhaps we should have left you in your house." He then added, ominously, "After we'd made sure you would not be able to betray us, that is."

Joseph had spoken very little during the last two hours, instead trying to conserve his strength for what was for him an arduous journey. He now said, "I know you have a grievance with me but Metjen has done you no ill. Let him now go free."

"And give him the opportunity to rush back to tell his master, who will then come chasing after us. No, we are not stupid, Joseph."

This was a noble gesture of this innocent

man whom I had come to respect, although a futile one. "I didn't expect any less of you three," I said. "But you'll be even more foolish if you set out in your boat now that the night will shortly be upon us."

"We don't intend to subject ourselves to the warring gods during the dark hours," Hepzefa said. "Instead we shall make a camp here, out of sight in the undergrowth, and will embark as soon as it's light. Two of us will be on guard throughout the night, so don't even think of trying to escape, Metjen."

It was clear that we had no alternative but to do as they wished. Our four captors ordered us to sit on the ground whilst they ate the food Theshen had collected from the house. When they'd eaten their fill they tossed the bag containing a few remaining morsels to Joseph and me. It was now dark and we lay down to try and rest, with two remaining on guard just as we had been told.

It was difficult to sleep, and I tried to review the options open to me. Should I suddenly dash into the cover of the trees and leave Joseph to try and cope on his own? As I knew the island well, I would stand a good chance of evading recapture. But then Theshen also resided here and had avoided the main routes when he guided us to the coast.

My other two house colleagues would

already be at home and would have realised something was wrong. Was Senusret also aware of this? If he was, had he already tried to find us? So many questions, but I must have dozed off because the next thing I was aware of were the first rays of Ra catching me in the eyes.

Chapter 9

The Hut

"Get up you two!" It was Hepzefa shouting his orders again. "Climb into the boat quickly; we're going to leave immediately." He had selected a vessel large enough to accommodate the man they hoped to catch as well as themselves, although he couldn't have anticipated there would be two extra passengers: Theshen and me. "Four men will row, and the other two will be on guard in case of any trickery."

Joseph and I took up our positions along with Neferu and my house mate who had turned traitor. "Joseph is an old man and you can't expect him to row a heavy boat like this for long," I said to Hepzefa.

"He will do what I tell him to do," he replied. "If he perishes with the effort it'll save us the job when we arrive at our destination."

"You are just being callous and cruel. Joseph didn't treat you like this in your earthly life," I couldn't prevent myself shouting out.

"That's not your business, and we still need to decide what to do with you, Metjen, when you are no longer of any use to us."

I remained silent, trying to save my breath for the effort of rowing. Poor Joseph was already suffering and was panting with every stroke of the oar. In between gasps he asked our main captor, "Where are we going? We are not heading directly for Flower Island."

"Indeed not," Hepzefa said. "We're going to bypass the intermediate islands and make directly for Lake Island where we live."

"But that'll take two days at least," I said angrily. "Do you expect us to row continuously, including through the night? We haven't eaten a proper meal for more than a day, except for the crumbs you threw at us last night."

"You will do what I say, like it or not. We shall waste time if we keep stopping, and I know you'll try to escape if we land anywhere else. I already said it will save us the effort if Joseph dies, and that's the same for you, Metjen. And I'm not concerned about being out in the open during the night; no harm will befall us."

What a foolish person he is, I thought, but resisted the temptation to agonise him further. We rowed on in silence. But, just as we were close to being out of sight of Arable Island, I saw two boats leaving the jetty and heading in our direction. Each looked to have at least six people on board. Could it possibly be that a party was coming to help us? Hepzefa hadn't seen these craft yet as he was facing forward guarding us as well as keeping us on his chosen direction. If the others had seen them they must have thought there was no need to mention it, but just concentrated on the effort of rowing.

An hour later Hepzefa called out, "Simontu and I will now relieve Neferu and Theshen. They will take over guard duties whilst we row."

"What about Joseph and me?" I asked. "We also desperately need to rest."

"You two will stay where you are," he replied. "I'm not so stupid as to let you alone with no one to guard you." There was no point in me arguing, because he would only repeat that he didn't care if we perished. But, as soon as he took his seat to row, he saw the two boats that were now gradually drawing closer to us.

"It looks like we're being followed," he announced. "We'll have to change course and make for Flower Island after all. If they also turn inland it'll confirm that the other boats are following us but, if we remain in the open sea, they'll eventually catch up with us." At least we shall not have to keep rowing overnight, I thought, even though it would still require more physical effort to reach land. If I do then have the chance to escape I shall try to reach Bebi and his companions.

Half an hour later we landed safely on Flower Island and, although exhausted myself, I had to almost carry Joseph onto the beach. "There's no time to rest. Move quickly into the trees," Hepzefa barked, ominously pointing his spear at us. With one arm supporting my companion, the two of us managed to stumble our way off the sand and into the undergrowth whilst the others dragged the boat into the undergrowth as far as they could to avoid it being seen.

If we still had any energy remaining we could have used this opportunity to dash inland but, in our present state we couldn't have gone a step further. "What shall we do now?" Theshen asked. "It does look as if the other boats have turned in our direction and I estimate they'll be here in little more than an hour."

"Yes, I didn't expect our presence to have been revealed so soon," Hepzefa conceded. "Someone must have seen us depart from Arable Island. We'll have to find a place to hide here and then set off again for our homeland when it's clear to do so."

Despite our pleas for some time to rest, Joseph and I were forced to start walking whilst again being guarded in front and behind. In order to avoid being seen we were ordered to avoid the main paths and make our way up hill through the rough undergrowth. Progress was slow, but deliberately made even slower by the two of us dragging our feet even more than we needed to. The shorter the distance we covered, then the greater the chance of us being found by those who were following us.

It was Theshen who broke the silence. "I'm hungry and need to stop and find something to eat. We've already passed some grape vines and trees bearing palm nuts. Let's take time to gather some."

"The longer we remain then the more chance we'll be caught," Hepzefa replied in an angry tone of voice. "I didn't think you would be as weak as our two prisoners are."

"I've worked hard to help you but now need to eat," Theshen said defiantly. How interesting, I thought, here is the first sign of what could become a significant breakdown in the relationship between my traitorous house mate and our captors.

"Very well," Hepzefa relented. "But be quick about it." Whilst he and Neferu kept guard over us, Theshen and Simontu went off to gather what food they could find. Joseph and I lay down to try and recover some of our strength. I peered through the gaps in the trees to see if there was any sign of others who might be following us, but could only see carpets of the colourful flowers that gave this island its name.

It wasn't long before the food party returned. Simontu carried some fruit and nuts but Theshen was yowling and shouting. In his hand he had a large piece of honeycomb but his face and arms were covered in red blotches. "I saw a bees nest in a tree and climbed up to it. Although I managed to grab this to eat, those darned insects stung me all over my bare flesh. I'm in agony!"

He didn't receive much sympathy from the others, and Joseph and I had difficulty restraining ourselves from laughing. Fortunately there was enough food for the two of us to receive a share, in contrast to last time. Whilst Theshen continued to moan about his pain, Hepzefa continuously urged us all to eat quickly so that we could be on our way again as soon as possible.

Eventually everyone rose to their feet and continued on through the wilder parts of the land, still keeping well clear of any paths. It made walking difficult, especially for Joseph who had only partly recovered from his exhaustion, and progress remained slow. I was sustained by the hope that those in the two boats were indeed Senusret and his men, and that they had landed and were caching up with us by using the main roads and paths.

As we walked I kept estimating how far we were from Queen Nefret's palace and the home of Bebi and Intef. If there was a chance to escape I could make my way back to the path and try to reach them for help. My captors would not know I had friends here. But then would it be right to involve them when they could also suffer at the hands of Hepzefa and the others? Perhaps they could ask the Queen for help. Whilst pondering these thoughts I became painfully aware of how much I missed the lovely Khumit. She was not even on this island now. Would I ever see her again, I wondered?

We spoke very little, each trying to conserve energy for the journey. But then we heard the sound of distant voices. Hepzefa called a halt whilst he listened to determine which direction the sound was coming from. It was behind us and to the left where the main path was. Could this be the people from the boats following us? I wondered. If so, maybe I could attract their attention.

It was clear that our captors were aware of my intention. "Move further to the right, away from the path" Hepzefa ordered. Reluctantly we obeyed. "Lay down on the ground you two," he said, indicating to Joseph and me. He then faced the other three: "Hold your spears against the throats of our prisoners and kill them if they make a sound. Everyone keep quiet until whoever it is has gone past."

The voices grew louder until they were level with us. I wished I could shout out but knew that it would be the last thing I uttered. The voices gradually receded and the opportunity was lost.

Hepzefa gave the order to continue once he was sure it was safe to do so, and we struggled on up the hill. As before, little was said and my thoughts returned to what I could do to help us out of this situation. If it was the Pharaoh and his men who had landed here, it's likely he was acquainted with Queen Nefret. She was not only his stepmother in his earthly life, but they were both now the senior officials of their respective islands. If I could only reach him, Senusret would be able to take control and defeat Joseph's enemies.

Once again it was Theshen who broke the silence with his shouting. "The afternoon is nearly over and it'll start to become dark before long," he said. "We don't want to be outside and exposed then."

"You are always complaining," Hepzefa replied. "I'm just as aware of our situation as you are, and I intend to see if there is any protection for us. Everyone look around as we walk, and speak up if you see anything we can use to shelter us for the night."

We continued on for another half hour. Just as we were becoming resigned to having to bed down in the open air we came across an overgrown path. It must have branched off from the main track somewhere to our left and continued on to the right. There, a short distance away, we saw a wooden construction that once may have been a store for agricultural equipment. Now clearly abandoned, it was in a poor state of repair. We walked toward it and Hepzefa ordered us to wait outside whilst he went in to have a look around.

"This is where we shall spend the night," he announced from the doorway. "It shouldn't take us long to block the gaps and make it secure. But before we start I want Simontu and Theshen to go quickly and see if there are any fruit trees nearby so we shall again have something to eat. Neferu and I will guard the prisoners whilst you are away."

"I'm still hurting from the bee stings from last time, so don't expect me to try and gather any more honeycomb," Theshen called out as, with obvious reluctance, he did as instructed. Within minutes the pair returned with a few items of fruit and nuts. But before we were permitted to eat anything, Hepzefa and Neferu went inside to carry out the necessary preparations to the shack.

"Right, everyone inside," Hepzefa

instructed, just as the last rays of light from Ra dipped below the horizon. We entered the gloomy interior and looked around as best we could. Apart from a few pieces of wood on the floor that had fallen from the decomposing roof, the building was empty.

"Go and sit on the ground in the corner where we can watch you whilst we eat our food," Hepzefa said. We did as he asked and, after our captors had satisfied their hunger, as before all we received were a few morsels of grubby leftovers. When they'd finished he said, "Two of us will again keep watch on you to make sure you don't try to escape during the night."

Joseph and I settled down as best we could on the hard, bare floor. Some light from the moon and stars shining through the gaps in the roof was the only illumination, but our eyes were growing accustomed to the gloom. We could just make out the shadowy figures of the other occupants. Hepzefa and Neferu lay down in the opposite corner to us, leaving Theshen and Simontu to take the first shift standing guard.

Although snoring from the other side of the room indicated that two of our captors had soon lapsed into unconsciousness, despite my tiredness I couldn't sleep. My mind persisted in reviewing our situation again and wondering whether or not Joseph and I could do anything about it. If there was an opportunity to escape during the night, would it be wise to take it? Because I'd visited this island before and, despite the darkness, I was sure I could find my way back to the main path and then onwards to the palace grounds where Bebi and Intef lived. But what if the warring gods saw me and attacked?

I wondered what Hepzefa was going to do next. His intention was to take us back to his home on Lake Island. Would he assume that it was Senusret and his men who had passed by earlier and were now ahead of us? If so, he'd want to return to the boat and continue onwards as quickly as possible. But could he be sure? Perhaps his vessel had been found and some of the guards had remained nearby so they could capture him and the others when they went back to it.

Although I may have dozed off for a short while, my eyes opened again. It was still dark but I could see the outlines of the others. Joseph had managed to go to sleep but something was not as expected. It took me a few seconds to realise what it was. Where were the two men who were supposed to be guarding us? I raised my head and saw them slumped on the floor asleep. They were no doubt as tired as we were and, with nothing to occupy them, had been unable to stay awake.

It hadn't been possible to properly secure the

door to this ruined store house. Should I use this opportunity to try and escape? It would mean that Joseph would be alone and at the mercy of our captors, but their intention was not to do away with him here but to take him back to their own island. If I could reach help then perhaps there would be a chance he could be saved. Yes, I concluded, that would be the best thing for me to do.

As quietly as I could I stood up and went to the door. Carefully opening it just far enough to squeeze through, I made my exit. There was no sound to indicate I'd been detected, so I gently pushed the door closed and stepped onto the overgrown track that would lead to the main path.

I realised I could be in danger if the gods decided to wage their war overhead, and there was barely enough light to see where I was going. Despite stumbling several times I managed to reach the path and then turned right up the hill. In the distance I heard the noise of the nightly battle. It came closer and I was sure I'd be seen but, fortunately, it soon receded and all was quiet again.

Although the walking was easier now that I was on a well-trodden track, the darkness sometimes caused me to wander into the undergrowth. After an hour the darkness started to fade and the gods would have returned to their homes. Knowing that Ra would soon be commencing his daily journey across the heavens gave me renewed energy. It wasn't long before I reached the top of the hill and saw the welcome sight of the royal palace on my left and Bebi's house on my right.

It would still be too early for my friends there to be up and about, and I wondered if I should wait before trying to attract their attention. But no, time was still of the essence if there was to be any chance of apprehending the evil ones and rescuing Joseph. I walked up to the door, knocked and waited. No response. I knocked again, harder this time. Eventually I heard a man's voice behind the door shouting "Who is it?"

"It is Metjen," I called out.

There was the sound of the bolt being drawn back and the door then opened just a small amount. "Stand where I can see you," he said. I did as asked, and the door immediately opened wide revealing the familiar figure of Intef, still clad in his night attire. "My goodness you're the last person I expected to see," he said. "I was concerned it was one of the warring gods trying to enter. Do please come right in and I'll call Bebi."

Once inside Intef secured the door again and went to fetch his colleague. We exchanged warm greetings and then Bebi asked: "What brings you back to us, especially so early in the morning?" I quickly summarised the events of the last few days. "It's clear that action needs to be taken as soon as possible to apprehend the villains and free Joseph. But did you know that Pharaoh Senusret and his men are at Queen Nefret's palace at this moment?"

"I did hear people walking up the hill yesterday but was unable to shout because there was a spear at my throat. I was hoping it would be them."

"As soon as I can get fully dressed we must quickly go over to the palace and inform your master. The sooner he can lead his men out to confront them and free Joseph the better will be the chance of success. You'll have to guide them to where they were hiding."

A few minutes later we crossed over the courtyard and up to the royal residence. It was still earlier than the time most people leave their bed, but we were soon admitted. We waited for what seemed a long time before being summoned into the guest room where Senusret was staying. I explained the situation and the need for speedy action if we were to have any chance of catching the villains.

"You have done well to escape and come to tell me this," Senusret said. "Fortunately you and your captors were seen by a fisherman as you were leaving Arable Island, and he had the presence of mind to immediately inform me. We followed as quickly as we could but then lost track of your party after your boat had landed. Our plan today was to search this island and question the inhabitants."

"Sir, I can guide you to the shack where we were encamped for the night. Although they might have departed when they discovered I'd escaped, we ought to be able to pick up their trail."

"Very well, Metjen, you go back to the house and I shall assemble my men. We shall collect you as soon as we are ready to leave here."

Bebi and I went back across the courtyard. "You must be both tired and hungry, and will shortly have to make the journey back down the hill," my friend said. "Sit down and rest until you are sent for. We'll make you something to eat to help you regain you strength." Indeed I was glad to have even this short time to try and refresh myself; the short sleep I had last night before escaping would not sustain me indefinitely.

No sooner had I managed to finish the first proper meal I'd eaten for what seemed a long time than a guard knocked on the door to inform me that the Pharaoh was ready to depart. I roused

my self from the chair and bid farewell to Bebi
and Intef, promising to come and see them again
when this mission was finally over. Joining my
master in front of the twelve guards he had
brought with him, we set off down the hill.

About an hour later we reached the
overgrown track that led to the dilapidated
storehouse. It was no surprise to find it was
empty. When my captors realised I had escaped,
they would have immediately departed, knowing
that I would be trying to obtain help. I just hoped
they were not taking their revenge out on Joseph,
but could imagine the anger that would have been
vented on the two guards who were supposed to
have been watching us.

"It is most likely the evil ones went back
down the hill to their boat," the Pharaoh said.

"Indeed sir you are surely correct. Even if
they'd assumed you and your men were not those
we heard yesterday, they'd have been foolish to
continue upwards where there are more people.
Their intention was to return to their own island
as soon as they could, and they only stopped here
to escape being caught by you when they saw you
following them."

"Then we must also make haste to where we
left our own two vessels. Maybe we can still
catch them," he said. We returned to the main
path and headed down to the sea. Because of my

previous exertions and shortage of both food and sleep, I had difficulty keeping up with the rest of the party. However, after another hour of marching we arrived at the landing site.

"Where are our boats?" Senusret exclaimed. "We left them tied up right here when we arrived yesterday."

I looked where Hepzefa had hidden the boat I came on, and it was also gone. "Sir, the party I came with has already departed. They must have set your boats adrift before they did so. But there are other craft further along the jetty for anyone to use. We can take two of those."

"Yes, we must do so as we cannot waste time. Maybe we shall find ours floating clear of the island once we are on our way, or perhaps they will have been washed up further along the beach."

The vessels available to us must have been smaller than the ones the Pharaoh had used to come here, because it was quite a squeeze fitting us all in. But it was a relief not being asked to take my turn rowing. The guardsmen were in a better physical condition than I was. "Were the rebels going to land on Animal Island?" Senusret asked, also free of rowing responsibility as might be expected for a royal personage.

"No sir, they intended to make us row direct from your island to their homeland without making landfall in between unless they had to."

"That would take more than one day and would put them at the mercy of the gods at night. It was a foolish aim," he commented.

We pulled away from the shore and, a few minutes later, a guardsman shouted: "I can see one of our boats there on the beach. The current must have carried it back to the shore. Shall we change course to retrieve it?"

Senusret called over to the other boat, "You row across and transfer into our boat, then tow the borrowed one back to the jetty and follow us. We shall continue on with this one."

No sooner had our sister vessel changed course to carry out the instruction than the Pharaoh's other boat was seen drifting in open water. My master then gave an order to the rowers in our vessel: "Change course to intercept it and tow it back to its mooring. We shall then exchange it for this one."

Oh dear, I thought, all this is going to waste us precious time. Eventually we were all back in the Pharaoh's more spacious boats, and the guards rowed us away in the direction of Animal Island. I could not prevent myself thinking again of the beautiful Khumit who was there being cared for by farmer Shakir and his wife Bennu. If only I could dive off this boat as we went past and swim ashore to be with her, leaving this mission for the others to complete. But of course I was in the service of Senusret and had to do his bidding.

We continued in silence, apart from grunts coming from the rowers due to their exertion. What the Pharaoh had said about the evil ones setting themselves the impossible task attempting to row all the way to Lake Island without stopping would surely also apply to us. The guardsmen were not machines but needed food and rest like all of us, and we were going to have to stop sometime.

It was after mid day by the time we were close to Animal Island. "Steer a course round the island and head for Lake Island," Senusret shouted so that those in the second boat also heard. I could hear subdued mutterings from the rowers but they didn't dare to question the order.

Just as we started to bypass the right side of the island one of the guards pointed to the shore and said: "Sir, there's a boat pulled up onto the beach; do you wish to investigate?" All eyes looked to where he was pointing. Although most of the vessels available for anyone to use are similar, there appeared to be something familiar about this one.

"This could be the boat that Hepzefa and his accomplices commandeered on your island when Joseph and I were their prisoners," I said. "They might have had to stop through exhaustion or the need for food. It may be fruitful if we went to investigate."

"I understand what you say Metjen," Senusret replied. "But if you are wrong then we shall have fallen even further behind those we are trying to catch."

"Although if they are there and we continue on our way without stopping, they'll be laughing at us from wherever they're hiding," I said. "Also, it'll give your own men a break and the opportunity to collect some food."

"Very well, but it will be your responsibility if you are wrong," the Pharaoh replied with lack of grace. "Make for the shore near to the craft on the beach," he barked at the rowers of both boats. They did so with renewed energy, obviously glad at this unexpected opportunity to have a break from their exertion. I searched carefully along the shoreline but could see no sign of any people. Was I wrong to try and persuade my master to deviate from his plan? We would shortly be able to find out.

Chapter 10

Boats at Night

As soon as my boat grounded on the shingle I leapt out, went over to the other vessel and looked inside. I was sure this was the one in which I was forced to row when we left Arable Island. Some food debris had been left scattered on the floor just as it was when my captors ate their last meal. I was therefore convinced the four villains and Joseph must be here somewhere.

Once the Pharaoh and his guardsmen had joined me on the beach I said, "Sir, those whom we are seeking will now be on this island; we must find them before they can carry out their vengeance on Joseph."

"Very well, but we shall not remain here for long unless we see evidence they are indeed here." Addressing his men he said, "Spread out and look for Hepzefa and the others. And while you are doing this gather any food that you see growing."

I joined in the search, looking for footprints along the beach that might indicate that five people had recently walked through the sand. Why did they stop here anyway? I wondered. Their original intention was to row non-stop from my home island to theirs, but this is the second time they've broken their journey. The first was when they saw the Pharaoh's boats following them. Could it be the same this time, or was there another emergency?

After an hour of searching one by one the guardsmen returned to where the boats were moored. "Have any of you caught sight of Joseph and his captors?" Senusret asked. The many footprints along the beach had made my attempt to identify any specific presence futile, and none of the others reported any clues as to their whereabouts.

"Metjen, you must have been wrong in your assumption, and we have let the evil ones have all this extra time to get further away from us," he said, adopting again the unfriendly tone reserved for addressing those he considered his inferiors. He continued, "It will be dark before long and I do not intend to set off again and be at the mercy of the gods. We shall eat the food that has been collected and then camp here until first light."

I joined the group and ate my share of the fruit and nuts, feeling rather despondent that I was responsible for the delay that might thwart our attempt to catch those we were seeking. But then, in the twilight, we all had a surprise. It was the very last thing we could have expected. Out from among the trees strode Hepzefa, Neferu, Simontu and Theshen. With them was Joseph stumbling along with his hands tied behind his back and a spear held at his throat.

"Greetings my friends," Hepzefa said in an arrogant voice. "How nice to see you all here. No, please don't rise up and approach; one move in our direction will result in this spear being pushed through Joseph's neck, and you will then hear his dying breath." Some of the guardsmen started to rise but the Pharaoh waved them to remain seated.

"That is most sensible of you, gentlemen," the evil one continued, obviously enjoying being the one dominating the situation. "We shall now board our boat and row away from here. If anyone tries to follow us this spear will do its work. Metjen, we shall also have the pleasure of your company, if you would kindly step this way."

"Why do you want me?" I asked. "You already have the man you've been seeking."

Hepzefa replied in the patronising tone he had adopted: "Ah, my dear friend, you've already caused us much trouble and will no doubt do so again if we leave you here. But we also need someone to share in the rowing. Just think how much help you and Joseph gave us before, and it will leave two of us to point our weapons in your direction at all times. Come and join us now, and no tricks or you and our other captive will both breathe your last."

I had no alternative but to comply, but wondered if the Pharaoh's men would risk rushing forwards to overpower the evil ones they outnumbered. But no, perhaps wisely in view of the risk to Joseph, they resisted. The light had almost gone by the time we'd boarded and pushed out into open water. Joseph had his hands untied but was clearly weak and suffering from his deprivations. As before, he and I were made to row, with two of our captors behind us and the others guarding us with their spears close to our faces.

"You're crazy to risk being on the sea during the night," I said between gasps from the physical exertion. "You know how dangerous it can be if the gods decide to conduct their nightly war games close to us."

"We shall be safe. Why should they wish to harm us when they had deemed us worthy to be resurrected and live here? But that would not stop them destroying you, Metjen as you are only a lump of stone brought to life to serve people like me." I was tempted to tell him what a despicable individual he was, but he was so puffed up with his self-importance that I'd have been wasting my time as well as the energy I needed to keep rowing. Instead I tried to think of ways Joseph and I might escape.

I wondered what Senusret was doing. If he was seen following us then there was no doubt that Hepzefa would carry out his threat. Maybe he would wait until daylight and then proceed to Lake Island without being detected. He and his men could then march to the home of the three evil ones and overpower them, but would we be still alive if he did? In any case I didn't know what the trio would do with Joseph even if they were not apprehended. Would they just make him a slave, or do away with him altogether?

My thoughts were interrupted by a familiar sound coming from the heavens. Yes, it was Ra waging his nightly battle against Seth, Ammut and rest of his antagonists. And it was coming closer to us. We were unprotected in the open sea, just as I had warned our captors, but their arrogance made them think they'd be invincible.

"Are you ready for the gods?" I couldn't resist calling out to Hepzefa.

"Shut up and row," he replied, using the superior tone he had recently adopted. "I've already told you they won't bother us."

The noise was now right overhead. Suddenly Ra was right there beside us. "Where are you taking Joseph and Metjen?" he asked our captors.

"Lord Ra, we are taking them to our home island because they have been troubling us," Hepzefa replied, now making some effort to adopt a more respectful voice.

"I know these people, and they have done nothing wrong," the god said. Release them now and take them back to their people."

"We shall not do that, sir. If you provoke us we shall use our weapons to dispense with them right here and now." Our four captors raised their spears aggressively, ready to strike us.

Ra stretched out his hand and directed a stream of energy toward each spear in turn. Sparks enveloped them and they were immediately dropped onto the decking as if they were red hot.

"Now throw them over the side," he said. "If you do not do so immediately, my energy will be directed at your bodies next time." The men realised they'd no alternative but to comply. "Very good. Now turn the boat around, relieve Joseph and Metjen from their rowing, and return to the island you have just left. There surrender yourselves to Pharaoh Senusret. When I am back in the heavens, I shall inform Osiris that the four of you must stand trial so that, if you are found guilty of disrupting the peace for which this Field of Reeds was created, your punishment will be determined by the forty-two judges."

Hepzefa must have realised that, should this happen, it was unlikely he and his accomplices would be found innocent. "Lord Ra, I regret that we will not comply with your order, but will instead take our chances and continue to our home on Lake Island."

On hearing this intention to defy him, the god stretched out his hand again and directed a stream of energy into the sea next to the boat. The water started to bubble. A swell formed so that the boat began to rock and then pitch up and down with ever increasing ferocity. It was obvious that, if this continued, we would shortly capsize. "Do you wish to try and swim back to the land, or remain in your vessel and proceed as I have directed?" Ra asked.

Knowing that the chances of reaching the shore swimming at night with all the potential dangers was ill advised, with obvious reluctance Hepzefa replied: "Very well, we shall row to where we started from and put ourselves into the hands of the Pharaoh. But we shall be found innocent of any crime if we are faced with a trial."

"I shall be watching your progress from above, and will inform Osiris that he will need to pass judgement on your actions" said Ra. "If you deviate from your intended course, I shall return to make sure that you do what you have promised." Addressing Joseph and me he added: "Be assured that, once you are back on the land, you will not be troubled this night by the battles up above." With that he was gone before his opponents in the heavens could catch him.

What a relief it was to be released from the burden of rowing and instead enjoy being ferried by those who, only a short while ago, were gloating over the discomfort Joseph and I were suffering. But this was the third time Ra had intervened to save me and my companions when it was most needed. I wondered again if it was just a coincidence, or whether he or someone was keeping a constant watch over us. However, I couldn't assume this would always be the case.

It wasn't long before, in the light provided by a silvery, waning moon, I could just make out two of the Pharaoh's men standing near one of their boats. They had probably been appointed to remain on guard whilst the others tried to rest. When they saw our boat approaching they must have alerted Senusret and his men because they were soon all standing there with weapons at the ready. Sure enough, as soon as we reached the shore they came forward ready to strike our captors.

I immediately stood up in the boat and shouted, "Stop! There'll be no need for fighting as the aggressors will surrender to you. I'll explain everything to the Pharaoh once we've all disembarked. Fortunately the guardsmen lowered their swords and spears, but kept them ready in case this was just a bluff. As soon as we were all on shore and the four evil ones had reluctantly submitted to being secured, I went across to where my master was observing the situation.

"This is a great surprise, Metjen. What caused you and your captors to return, and so soon after you had departed?"

"My Lord, the God Ra had observed what was happening and broke away from his nightly battle to help Joseph and me."

"You were honoured that he regarded you both so important as to risk his own capture in order to intervene on your behalf," he replied with perhaps just a hint of envy.

"Yes sir, but this was not the first time; he had previously done so on two previous occasions even before I had found Joseph. He may have maintained an interest in my quest after those I was with at the time provided him with shelter during one of his skirmishes with the other gods."

"Now that Joseph is safely back with us, and the evil ones have surrendered, did your new friend Ra give you any further instructions?" Senusret asked.

"He told me that the three of them, plus the shabti Theshen, will be put on trial by Osiris, and their fate determined by the panel of judges. We shall soon be rid of them and be able to return to our peaceful life here."

"That is good," he said, but was there a suggestion of regret behind this? He'd asked me to embark on this mission so he could engage in some military action, but it seemed now that all he has had to do was guard some prisoners. Once this episode was over, I wouldn't be surprised if he asked me to go out again to find something to satisfy him.

"Then there is little for us to do now but wait for Osiris," Senusret commented quietly. "But being out here unprotected we remain vulnerable to the gods."

"Ra assured me that we shall not be troubled tonight as he'll make sure the battles continue far from here," I said. "We can therefore relax and try to rest until morning."

"Very well, Metjen. Our prisoners will not escape whilst their hands and feet are tied, but I shall instruct my men to guard them during the night whilst we sleep."

It was good to know this adventure was nearing its completion and that we could now have some untroubled rest. Two guardsmen remained on watch whilst we made ourselves as comfortable as we could on the grass at the edge of the beach. Except for the gentle swishing sound of the waves it was quiet and peaceful, and my eyes were losing their will to keep me awake.

As I drifted into slumber my thoughts returned to my dear Khumit who was at this moment right here on this island. Would I have the opportunity to leave the Pharaoh and his men to complete the mission by themselves now that everything appeared to be under control, and go to see her?

* * *

I became aware of people shouting. Was I dreaming? I opened my eyes. It was daylight and some of the guardsmen were clearly agitated.

"Pharaoh, the prisoners have gone and two of our men are injured," someone called out anxiously. I immediately got up and joined the others who had gone over to investigate. Indeed the three evil ones were no longer there, but Theshen remained with his limbs still tied. Two of the guards were lying on the ground groaning and I could red patches of blood on their heads.

"What happened here?" Senusret asked, clearly angry.

"Sir, I saw it all," Theshen replied. "We remained awake waiting for you all to go to sleep. The two men guarding us sat down and we could see that their heads were starting to droop."

"They will be disciplined for their negligence," the Pharaoh bellowed. "But how did the other three escape?"

"Simontu managed to wriggle his hands free from the bonds and then quietly slid close to the other two and loosened theirs. They then each untied the ropes from their feet. I waited for him to do the same for me, but I was ignored."

"What happened to the two men who have been injured?"

"Hepzefa and Neferu slowly reached out their hands and picked up lumps of rock from among those scattered around the beach, and together brought them down heavily onto the backs of the guard's heads. They slumped onto the ground without making a sound."

I could see from Senusret's face that his fury was increasing. "Why did they not also release you?" he asked.

"Sir, they just looked at me with contempt, and picked up the spears the guards had dropped. They told me they would slit my throat if I called for help, and then walked away into the surrounding woods as silently as they could."

The Pharaoh turned toward the remaining

guardsmen. "You ten men come with me," he shouted. "We are going to find these rebels and bring them back to stand trial. They cannot be far away. Joseph and Metjen, you stay here and do what you can for the injured men."

Moments later they were gone and the two of us bent down to see if we could help the fallen guards. They were still alive but obviously in pain. Tearing some strips off our clothing we bandaged their wounds as best we could and raised them into a sitting position. "What should we do about Theshen – shall we untie him?" Joseph asked, looking at the now forlorn figure of the man who had once been a trusted house mate of mine.

Before I had the chance to respond, Theshen spoke up. "I've been very foolish, carried away with the thought that I would be given an important position by Hepzefa and his accomplices. They never intended to honour their promise but just used me until I was no longer of use to them."

"Yes, Theshen, you have indeed been foolish," I replied. "But how can we trust you now? Perhaps you're just playing games with us and will change allegiance again when you have the chance."

"I do understand," he said. "All I can do is repeat my regrets and promise that I'll do all I can to help you both."

"Joseph, what do you think?" I asked. "Should we believe what he says and release his bonds?"

"He seems to be speaking with sincerity and yes, I would release him. There may come a time when we shall be glad of his help. But what will your master say if he returns and finds the prisoner has been freed?"

"Yes, that's a consideration," I replied." But I'll accept the responsibility for doing so."

We untied the ropes from Theshen's hands and feet. He massaged his numbed limbs to try and restore some feeling. "Thank you both," he said. "I shall not let you down."

There was little to do now but wait with the hope that the Pharaoh and his men would capture the evil trio, but I had to admit that we were vulnerable out here on our own without any protection. Ra was now high in the heavens and I was just about to go and see if I could find some fresh water to quench our thirst when we heard voices. The guardsmen must be returning, hopefully with their three prisoners.

Out from the bushes strode three men. They were Hepzefa, Neferu and Simontu, and they were alone. "I can see you are surprised to see us, my friends," Hepzefa said mockingly.

"Our little trick deceived your ignorant

Pharaoh and his men. All we had to do was hide nearby, knowing that the search party would think we would be much further away by now. The fools did just what we had suspected."

"You will not succeed with this," I answered. "They'll be back here at any moment and you'll be prisoners again, awaiting your trial."

"Not so," he replied. "We shall leave immediately, taking just Joseph with us this time, all tied up and helpless. The sea is calm and we shall reach our own island before nightfall. Your Pharaoh will not be in a hurry to wage war on the entire population there." They started walking toward us. "Get into our boat, Joseph, or we'll do away with you right here"

Theshen sprang to his feet and stood in front of Joseph, shouting: "No, you shall not do this. You deceived me into believing your promise of reward, but I can see now that you never intended to keep it. I shall prevent you taking this innocent man away from here."

Hepzefa continued to come forward, brandishing the spear he had taken earlier from the guard. "But you are not armed, my friend, and I have this." Theshen held his position with the point of the spear pointing directly at his chest. "Move out of the way immediately or you'll be like a fish wriggling on the end of a harpoon."

"You'll then have to contend with me," I said, wondering if it would be possible to bluff this out until help arrived.

"But there are three of us with two spears, and we shall have no regrets if you both perish, and that goes also for Joseph if he tries to intervene. Well Theshen, are you going to move, or just remain there like a dumb statue?"

He did not move, and Hepzefa thrust his spear forward. Theshen fell to the ground, blood seeping through his tunic. I started to move but there were two spears directed at me. "Just keep going, Metjen, and we can then finish the job." But, before I made a decision, Hepzefa suddenly fell to the ground. One of our injured guardsmen had kicked out with his feet and caused him to lose his balance.

I took the opportunity to quickly grab his spear and turned to face Neferu who was holding the other one. Simontu, although unarmed, advanced toward me. Could I defeat them both? If Joseph could just grab hold of Neferu's spear we might have a chance. For a second or two everyone remained still as each waited for the other to make the first move. It did look like I would be on the losing end of this confrontation. Should I just pull back and let the evil ones have their way? We might yet have a later chance to apprehend them.

"Drop your weapons!" came a shout from the undergrowth. It was the Pharaoh. He and his men had returned sooner than our adversaries had expected. They quickly approached, overpowered Neferu and secured all three of our enemies. "Hepzefa, you did not fool us for long," Senusret said. "We knew you would not want to penetrate deep into the countryside whilst it was dark, so we soon doubled back and found you here. Just as well we did, in view of what you were about to do."

"I'm certainly glad to see you my Lord," I said with relief. "The rebels would soon have departed with Joseph, but I fear that Theshen is mortally wounded. He realised how wrong he had been and then tried to protect Joseph."

"That is unfortunate," the Pharaoh replied. "He should have had the chance to express his regrets when giving evidence at his trial. Perhaps he might have received clemency from the judges. All we can do now is make sure these three evil ones do not escape again and then wait for Osiris to arrive." Addressing two of his men he said, "Go and find some more food so that we can sustain ourselves until the trial begins."

We made Theshen as comfortable as possible, but his life was ebbing away. After ensuring that our captives had no opportunity to escape again, there was little more to do but sit, eat some of the fruit the guards had gathered, and wait for Osiris to arrive.

Chapter 11

The Trial

It was midmorning before Osiris, the God of Death and the Underworld suddenly appeared. "I am here to conduct the trial of three resurrected men and one shabti who have all been accused of violating the rule of peace and tranquillity for which this Field of Reeds was created," he said with an authoritative tone of voice. "You will not see the forty-two judges who will decide the outcome, but they can hear all that takes place."

This was the first time any of us had seen this sinister member of the community of gods. Although he and the judges weigh the hearts of those who have enjoyed an earthly existence to determine if they are worthy of resurrection, this is rarely witnessed. Osiris had an appearance commensurate with his appointed duties. His hands and bearded face were green, which contrasted with the white robe partially mummy-wrapped at his legs. He wore a distinctive crown, and in his hands he carried a symbolic crook and flail. These objects were respectively associated with kingship and the fertility of the land.

He spoke again: "Hepzefa, Neferu and Simontu, what do you have to say in the defence of the charges directed at you?"

As usual it was Hepzefa who was the first to answer. "My Lord Osiris, I have not willingly committed any sin against this paradise. It was the other two who made me join them in taking revenge against an innocent man who they said had aggrieved them during their earthy life. I had to reluctantly agree otherwise I'd have also been a victim of their wrath."

This complete fabrication of the truth caused me and some of the others to gasp; surely Osiris wouldn't believe him. He continued with his testimony. "I was a good friend of Joseph when we both served at the court of Pharaoh Senusret the Second, and regarded him as a wise counsellor. He deserves to enjoy his time here in the afterlife. That is all I have to say at this time."

The god then addressed Neferu. "What do you have to offer in your defence?"

"Sir, what Hepzefa has just said is grossly untrue. He was the organiser of this mission to hunt down and punish Joseph. We were all members of the same court but Joseph was appointed Viceroy over our heads. Hepzefa was the most aggrieved of all of us but was powerless to take any action because it would have gone against the Pharaoh's wishes."

"Very well," Osiris said. "Now let us hear from Simontu."

"My Lord, I agree with my colleague Neferu. It was Hepzefa who instigated this attempt to take vengeance on Joseph. But we all resented his appointment, especially as he was a foreigner and we'd been loyal citizens of Egypt. One of us should have been given the appointment instead of him."

"Very well, I have heard your testimonies. Now it is the turn of Joseph."

"Lord Osiris, I do not wish to speak out against my fellow resurrected ones," he said quietly and with dignity. "I have spent the last year travelling and encountered many kind people who have helped me. When I reached Arable Island I met Metjen, who then introduced me to Pharaoh Senusret. He offered me sanctuary and then led a party of his men to find and banish those who had been trying to apprehend me."

I shouldn't have been surprised to hear such complaisant words coming from this man, but it was no doubt indicative of the way he had conducted his duties at the royal court. He continued: "Whilst the Pharaoh was away, the three who have spoken already came to visit and said they would take me to their home on Lake

Island. But we had many diversions along the way, and never reached it. That is all I have to say."

I wondered if Osiris would now think that the three men were innocent of any crime, and allow them to be released without any punishment. He pointed his crook in the direction of my master and said, "Pharaoh Senusret, would you like to say something?"

"Indeed I would," he responded. "I sent my Viceroy, Metjen, out on a tour of this land to see if there were any indications of rebellion or dispute that could disturb the peaceful existence of its inhabitants."

But Osiris was not so easily deceived. "So you intended to take it upon yourself to act as watchdog and maintainer of law and order. And what would you have done if you had discovered any of these misdemeanours?"

"Sir, I would have tried to quell them for the good of everyone who wishes to enjoy this paradise that you and your fellow gods have created for us."

"But do you not think this is a task best left to the gods themselves to perform?"

I could see that Osiris was being a sceptical about my master's true motivation. "Of course I had no intention of taking on your role, but just wished to make myself useful and avoid you having to concern yourselves with trivial matters that I could easily resolve for you."

"That is most considerate of you, Senusret," the god replied with more than a hint of sarcasm. "But, if you have more ideas like this, just make sure you do not exceed the authority that has been given to you in this afterlife. But now tell me what you know about the three me who are on trial."

"Metjen brought Joseph to see me after he had found him hiding on my island trying to escape from those who are standing before you now. He had served my father well, but it is true there were those who resented a foreigner like him being promoted above them. Whilst they were unable to take action against him during their earthly lives, they intended to do so now."

"So what action did you take when you heard this?" Osiris asked.

"I called together some of my own men and we went to seek out those who were trying to catch Joseph. When we returned later in the day I discovered that he had been taken captive along with Metjen. I was determined they must be saved from these evil ones so, early the next morning, we set off once more to find them. We eventually landed here and captured them all."

"Very well, Senusret, I am sure I can piece together what happened next. But let us hear from

Metjen, the one you sent out on this mission."

"Thank you for the opportunity to speak, my Lord," I began. "Yes, it's as you've already been told. I firstly spoke to many on my own island, but they had nothing to report. When I reached the shore I met some people who were from Flower Island. They had come to collect food to take back to the court of Queen Nefret. Once I'd informed them of my mission, they told me about Joseph and how he was trying to evade capture by the men who are on trial."

"I see," said Osiris. "So what did you do next?"

"I joined them on the journey back to Flower Island. The next morning three of them agreed to accompany me on my travels to find Joseph so that I could offer him the protection of my master. We visited other islands without success. I only discovered him when I returned home, and Pharaoh Senusret then offered him sanctuary. However, we were betrayed by Theshen and both of us were taken prisoner by the accused."

"How did you end up here on Animal Island," the god asked.

"We had many adventures but it was Ra who intervened when our situation was bad," I continued. "Even this morning you could have arrived and found that the three evil ones had gone, along with Joseph. Fortunately we managed to succeed in taking them prisoner."

"Just one final question," Osiris said. ""What were the men going to do with Joseph once they had taken him back to their own island?"

"From the contemptuous way they were treating him, I'm sure they'd have either made him as a slave or done away with him altogether. They had no qualms about killing Theshen once he was of no further use to them."

"Then I shall let the judges reach their verdict. They have heard what you have each testified and have all the evidence they need."

"My Lord, may I just make a plea to be merciful toward Theshen," I asked. "Yes, he did betray us to the rebels, but his mind had been poisoned by the thought he'd be given an important position by the evil ones. It was only later he realised he was being deceived. He was courageous in protecting Joseph and taking the spear that was intended for him."

"The judges will also have heard this," Osiris answered. "We must now leave it to them to deliberate and inform of their decisions."

I wondered how long this would take, but we just had to sit down and wait. After an hour Osiris announced that the verdicts had now been conveyed to him. "The hearts of Hepzefa, Neferu and Simontu have been weighed and each found to be heavier than a feather. Instead of respecting the peace for which this Field of Reeds was created, they have been intent on taking revenge on an innocent man. They will therefore be removed from this place and delivered into the hands of the God Ammut, devourer of the dead. They will never again be a threat to those residing in this afterlife."

"No, you can't do this to us," Hepzefa cried out. "We are innocent of any crime." But that was the last we saw or heard of them, as their images slowly faded from our sight.

Osiris continued. "The judges had heard your plea for clemency for Theshen. He will not be ground into dust as are those considered unworthy, but will be transformed back into the stone shabti he was before being brought to life to serve his Pharaoh. When it is considered appropriate for him to be made alive again to serve another resurrected one, he will once more become an inhabitant of this world."

"I'm pleased that the judges came to this decision," I said. "He was a good servant before his mind was distorted by the evil ones."

Osiris nodded in acknowledgement and then stretched out his arm toward the prone figure of Theshen. My ex house mate faded from view just as the evil ones had done, and was now free of suffering. The god then turned to address my master. "Pharaoh Senusret, the judges have asked me to give you a message"

"I am surprised, as I did not think I was one of those to be put on trial," he replied. "What would they want with me?"

Ignoring a direct response to this question, the god said: "They acknowledge that, in this case, you played a part in preventing those three rebels from violating the peace for which this land was formed. However, they wish to caution you against disturbing the tranquillity yourself in order to satisfy your enjoyment of military campaigns."

"I shall certainly keep this in my mind at all times," he replied. "But I do assure you that my wish was not for any personal gratification; it was only to prevent an injustice." I was amused that Osiris and the judges were fully aware of the behaviour of my master, as they were when he was originally considered for resurrection. Would this latest reminder really curb his desire for action? I had my doubts that it would.

"The judges have completed their report and departed," Osiris said. "But I now wish to speak with you, Joseph."

"I am ready to hear what you have to say, my Lord," he answered.

"You are indeed a virtuous man who has been unfairly persecuted by those who were jealous of your position in your earthly life.

When you served your Pharaoh as Viceroy you performed your duties with wisdom, fairness and compassion. Now that Hepzefa and his associates are no more, there is a need for a Senior Citizen to guide the inhabitants of Lake Island. I invite you to take on this role and live in the palatial house there."

Joseph's face lit up in a way I not seen before. "Sir I am honoured to be offered this position. In my previous existence I tried to be a worthy administrator and will do the same again. I am pleased to accept your invitation."

"That is good. My work here is finished," Osiris said. His image then disappeared as quickly as it had arrived.

Senusret now regarded himself as being in command again. He indicated to two of his guardsmen. "I want you to take Joseph to Lake Island and stay a while help him to settle in to his home. When this is done you are to return to my service."

On hearing this Joseph came across to speak with us. "I want to thank you most sincerely for all you have done to save me from the relentless persecution I have had to endure from those vindictive three men. Metjen risked his life for me and I regret that one person died who would not have done so if this had never happened. I shall always be grateful to you all. May the blessings of all the gods be upon you."

This was a touching speech, but added to the satisfaction as well as relief that the act of aggression was now over. There were times when I doubted we would succeed, and we were fortunate that Ra became aware of our situation and intervened at crucial moments. "I wish you well, Joseph," I said. "I shall come to visit you when I am able." We embraced each other in fellowship and he then left to join the men who would take him home.

"Well Metjen, it looks like this episode is now over and justice has been done. We can now return to our own island," Senusret said. "I have enjoyed this diversion from my routine existence, and we must discuss what future missions I can undertake to fulfil my intention to police this afterlife."

Oh dear, I thought, my master has gained nothing from the caution he received from Osiris only minutes ago. "Indeed sir we can do so, if you're sure that is what you wish."

"You have served me well, and it is fitting that as my Vizier you come to live in the palace," he continued as if he had not heard my response. "I shall have rooms prepared for you as soon as we are back home."

"Thank you sir, that will be a privilege," I replied. "But before we leave there is a request I wish to make to you."

"And what might that be?"

"One of the three friends from Flower Island who informed me about Joseph's plight and then accompanied me during most my mission is a woman. I have developed a great affection for her. Because of her exhaustion we had to leave her on this island in the care of a local farmer. With your permission I'd like to delay my homeward journey and go and see her."

"Ah, so you have found a lady friend," Senusret replied with a jovial tone unusual for him. "Very well, Metjen, you may go and visit her. Come and see me when you return."

"Thank you sir. If I leave now I'll be at the farmer's house before it's dark. Then tomorrow I can take her back to her own island where she serves Queen Nefret."

Remembering our encounter with the lion when I was here before, I went over the picked up one of the spears that had been dropped by the evil ones. As there was nothing more to discuss with the Pharaoh, I made my way to the main path and started to walk up the hill toward where Shakir and his wife Bennu lived. It will be so nice to be with Khumit again, I thought, and I hope she is still safely in their care and in good spirits. By late afternoon I arrived at the farm gate.

There in the front yard was their large,

brown dog Tut. When he saw me he came bounding toward me, wagging his tale in friendly greeting.

The door opened and a face peered out to see what had distracted Tut. It was Shakir, and he immediately turned round and called to someone inside. A figure appeared. It was Khumit. She ran toward me whilst I opened the gate to let myself in to the yard. Throwing her arms around my neck she kissed me and said, "Oh Metjen, I wondered if I'd ever see you again. We heard there'd been trouble down at the coast and I feared you had been taken by the evil ones."

I assured her that I was well although there had been some danger. "Let's go inside and I'll explain everything to you all," I said. We went into the farm house with Khumit's arm in mine, and I greeted Shakir and Bennu. Once we were all comfortably seated I gave everyone a summary of my adventures since we'd last been together. "The evil ones have now met their fate and Joseph has been appointed Senior Citizen of Lake Island in their place. This mission is finally over," I concluded.

Everyone was pleased to hear this and to know that I was safe. "I can now take you back to your home on Flower Island," I said to Khumit.

"I thought that eventually this would be the case," Shakir commented. "She's been a great help to us and has more than earned her stay here."

"Yes, we've grown fond of Khumit and will miss her," added Bennu. "I hope we shall meet both of you again during your travels."

"I'll also miss you both and your kindness, and of course we'll try to visit you as often as we can," Khumit said. "But it's only right that I now return to my home and continue to serve Queen Nefret."

"Yes, I do understand. But let us now make something to eat and we can continue to chat over the meal," said Shakir. "You will need to build up your strength before you depart tomorrow. If you intend making the whole journey in one day you'll need to make an early start."

I realised I'd not enjoyed a full meal for several days, so the delicious fare plus mugs of home-brewed beer that our hosts served were most welcome. Eventually all the questions had been answered and tiredness caught up with me. We retired to our beds and I spent a restful night safe from the distant rumblings from the heavens that reminded me how much we owed to the gods who were now enjoying their nightly ritual.

Just as Shakir had said, we needed to be on our way as soon as Ra had once again lit up the heavens. We bade fond farewells to our hosts, whose final gesture was to give us some food for our journey and, after giving Tut a pat on the head, made our way down the hill to the sea.

"You know, whilst I'm so pleased to be going home, I've enjoyed my stay with these farmers," Khumit said. "They helped me to recover when you had to leave me, and treated me as if I were one of their family. I do hope we can visit them again sometime."

"If Senusret sends me out on more missions and you are with me, I'm sure we shall come to this island again," I replied. Her response was to just give my hand a squeeze, and we continued onwards whilst keeping a watchful eye out for dangerous animals. Two hours later we safely reached the jetty and I selected one of the smaller boats. "We've made good time and should arrive at Flower Island early in the afternoon if we have no mishaps."

The sea remained calm and we made land as I'd predicted. "We can rest now for a short while and enjoy what our farmer friends have packed up for us. Do you think you have the energy to walk up to the palace so that we arrive there before dark?" I asked.

"I'm sure I can manage; working for the farmers has made me stronger. But let's now just sit down and enjoy our food," she said.

We continued our journey once we'd finished eating. Neither of us said much, partly because walking up hill required more effort. But I was trying to come terms with a feeling that was starting to grow stronger the nearer we became to the palace, and I wondered if Khumit was experiencing the same. We eventually passed the overgrown path that led to the shack that had sheltered Joseph and me, along with our captors, and I pointed this out to my companion.

The palace eventually came into view as Ra had almost completed his journey across the sky. We walked toward the home where my friends lived and knocked on the door. It opened to reveal the figure of Bebi. He stood for a moment as if trying to be sure that what he was seeing was not an illusion, before giving us a big grin. "Welcome back both of you; come in quickly so that I can bolt the door."

Everyone came to greet us and a few tears of joy were shed. Eventually we all sat down and Bebi said, "We didn't expect to see you back here, so please tell us what happened. The last we knew was when Metjen and the Pharaoh set off down the hill to try and catch up with the evil ones who were holding Joseph captive. Were you successful?"

"We had adventures along the way and at one time we thought we'd failed," I replied. "But once again the gods intervened. The evil ones are no more and Joseph has been appointed Senior

Citizen of Lake Island in their place."

After I'd answered the many questions that followed, Khumit said, "Metjen then revisited the farm where I'd been left, and brought me home. Tomorrow I shall go to the palace and tell the Queen that I am now able to resume my service with her."

"And I must return to my own island and do my Pharaoh's bidding," I added.

"Let's talk more about this tomorrow," Bebi said. "But now is the time to celebrate. We shall go and prepare a feast to welcome your return. You two just rest a while whilst we make the food."

The others went into the kitchen and left us alone. Khumit started to cry softly. "What's the matter, my dear?" I asked, going over to her chair and putting my arm around her shoulder.

"As we were walking back I kept thinking that you would soon be leaving us," she said between sobs. "I was longing for the day when we'd together again, but it'll only be for a brief time before you have leave for your own home."

"My thoughts are the same as yours," I replied. "Khumit, I want you to come back with me and be my wife. Will you marry me?"

"Oh yes, yes, I will!" she shouted, flinging her arms around me.

"I hear loud talking," Intef said standing in

the doorway. "Is there anything wrong?"

"No, nothing wrong; we are going to be married," Khumit announced. The rest of the household soon joined us, offering their congratulations. "When I see the Queen tomorrow I shall have to ask her if she will release me from her service. I can't just leave without her consent because I was created to serve her."

We didn't concern ourselves any more about that during the evening, but just enjoyed a celebratory meal with our friends, with perhaps a little too much of the local brew.

The next morning we had the more serious business to attend to. As soon as she'd broken her fast Khumit went across to the palace to discuss her situation with the Queen. I waited anxiously to see what the outcome would be. It wasn't long before my future wife returned with a smile on her face. "Good news, Metjen. Queen Nefret said that the girl who had replaced me during my absence had performed well, and that she can now stay permanently. But I should offer myself for service to your Pharaoh."

"That's wonderful," I said. "Your mistress is very kind and I'm sure Senusret will find that you are a worthy addition to his staff."

"There is more," Khumit continued. "She says she'll be happy to conduct the marriage ceremony for us this afternoon, so we can then go to your island as husband and wife."

"This is all happening very quickly, but it will be a marvellous conclusion to this mission after all the dangers we've been through," I responded. "Let's tell the others and then we can all make ourselves ready for the ceremony."

The wedding later that day was a joyous affair, and all Khumit's household were able to attend. When the ceremony was over, the Queen provided us with yet another celebratory meal. We returned to the house and continued our rejoicings until tiredness caught up with us and we retired for the night. Yesterday had started with feelings of sadness, but today has ended in happiness.

There were emotional farewells the next morning as we departed, although we knew that Bebi, Intef and the others often came to Arable Island to collect farming produce for the palace kitchens. There would be many opportunities for us to meet them again.

As I walked down the hill hand in hand with the woman I loved, I wondered what the Pharaoh would say when I arrived back not alone but with my bride. It would probably not surprise him, in the light of his comments when he allowed me to make this diversion instead of joining him on his return journey. I also wondered what devious schemes he might be hatching in order to satisfy his desire to be the keeper of the peace. No doubt I would soon find out.

- - - - - - - - - - - - -

Printed in Great Britain
by Amazon